# DREAM BIG

## THE SABLE SERIES - BOOK 8

## TINA HOGAN GRANT

TINA HOGAN GRANT BOOKS

# CHAPTER 1

## SABELA

"Hi Sabela, it's Claire. I have something for you."

I was sitting at the kitchen counter in my white bathrobe drinking my second cup of coffee when Claire called. Hope and Joy were sleeping in their cribs upstairs. I couldn't believe they'd just turned six months old. Where had the time gone? Scottie, Slater's biological son from Eve, was almost six and had left for school with Slater ten minutes ago. The condo was finally quiet, and I was absorbing every precious minute, because I knew as soon as the girls woke up, my day would no longer be my own.

I squealed into the phone, jumping up and down like an excited child. "Is it here?" I asked, unable to control my excitement.

"Yes, it is. When do you want to come by?" Claire replied, giggling at my high-pitched voice.

Tears pooled in my eyes. Slater and I had been waiting for this moment, wondering when it would arrive, and it finally had. My heart raced as I spoke, and I rested my hand on my chest to try and calm myself. "If it were up to me, I'd jump in my car right now and race over to your place, but I want Slater and Scottie to be with me. This is a special family moment, and we should all be together," I told her.

"I couldn't agree more," Claire replied in a caring voice. I sensed her smile. She was excited for us. "When would be a good time?" she asked.

"Slater and Ricky are putting in a bid for a condominium complex this morning. He was going to pick up Ricky after dropping Scottie off at school, but I'm not sure how long he will be. Can I call you after I hear from him?"

I laughed at Claire's high-pitched reply: "Wow, you guys are doing the big jobs now!"

"Business has really taken off. No more small remodels for us. We hired a crew of 15, and Slater made Ricky foreman."

"I heard. Jill told me last week and she's so excited," Claire laughed. "She said that he comes home every night and does nothing but talk about his new position and the responsibilities. The best part is, he hasn't played a video game since his promotion." Claire laughed again. "Jill said that it's like he's grown up overnight."

I joined Claire in her laughter. "Oh, that's funny. She always used to complain about how he'd come home and immediately start playing video games and not pay attention to her. Well, I'm glad we were able to help. How is she working out at the children's home?"

"She's fantastic. I had no idea how good she was around kids; I don't think she knew either, but all the children love her. Especially the eldest, Jasmine. They have a special bond. When Jasmine first arrived here, she was so quiet and withdrawn; I'm sure she was scared too, but she warmed up to Jill immediately, and when she found out Jill's favorite color was pink, she found a connection and they really hit it off. Jill helped decorate her room with sparkly girly accessories, and pink bedding and curtains. It turned out really cute."

"Oh, that's wonderful. And what about you, Claire? How are

you doing? I haven't seen you in over a week. Every time we talk, it's business. How is the pregnancy going? I hope you're not overexerting yourself. Slater and I have told you; if you need to hire extra help, we're okay with it. We may own the house and the business, but you and Travis are one hundred percent in charge of running the place. We leave all the decisions up to you."

"I appreciate that Sabela, but Jill and Travis' mom Caroline are a tremendous help, and of course Travis, too. They're doing everything, including making sure I stick to my diet, take walks every day and get plenty of rest. My mom, by the way, is doing an amazing job in the kitchen. I'd forgotten how good of a cook she is. Her meals are incredible. And the best part is, she's having fun and smiling again. I'm so happy we were able to make amends, and that she's now a part of my life again. It was the best decision to include her in this adventure and make her a part of the children's home."

"That's so good to hear, Claire, after all that you and your mom have been through. You did the right thing making amends with her."

"Yeah, I treated her badly. Our relationship isn't perfect: I know that we're both carrying a tremendous amount of guilt, but we're working through it, and I owe it all to our miracle baby. If it weren't for me getting pregnant, I'm not sure if our relationship could have been saved."

"I'm so happy for you and Travis, and it can only get better from here. And what about you? Are you feeling okay?"

I pictured Claire rubbing her stomach as she spoke. "Only four more weeks and I'll be through the first trimester. I'm not going to lie - Travis and I have been a nervous wreck since we found out I was pregnant. They told us that because I have PCOS, there's a substantial risk of me losing the baby during the first trimester. If that happens it'll destroy us both. I'll feel somewhat relieved when the first trimester is behind me."

The fear in Claire's voice was undeniable. "Don't go there

Claire," I told her in a firm voice. "As long as you've been doing what the doctors tell you, I'm sure everything will be okay."

"I'm feeling good. I get tired more easily and often, but when I do, I make sure to stop what I'm doing and rest." She chuckled, which I was pleased to hear. "We're doing everything by the book and seeing our obstetrician once a week. I just wish this month would speed up and be behind us. I feel like I can't relax until I'm past the first trimester. You must have been a nervous wreck when the twins were born six weeks early?"

"Oh, we both were. I know the fear you're going through, and I wish I could erase it all for you, but you're being closely monitored, and if they had any reason to be alarmed, they'd tell you."

Claire released a heavy sigh, "I know. I'm just counting the days to the second trimester, but even then we might not be out of the woods. My obstetrician also told me that having PCOS puts me at risk of developing high blood pressure or even gestational diabetes later in the pregnancy. So, they'll be monitoring me for that throughout the entire pregnancy."

"It sounds like you're in good hands and they're on top of it. Try not to let the worry consume you, okay?"

Claire released a nervous laugh, "I'm trying. Keeping busy really helps and takes my mind off it. Taking care of six kids is certainly keeping me busy," she chuckled. "Anyway, your final adoption papers are here. They've been approved and you're officially Scottie's mom. Congratulations!" Claire squealed.

"Oh, thank you, Claire. I can't wait to tell Slater," I told her, my eyes welling up with tears. "Can we come by this afternoon after we've picked Scottie up from school?"

"Of course. Come by whenever you want. I'll be here all day; I don't get much free time with six kids in the house," she joked.

I laughed. "You certainly have your hands full."

"I do, but Travis and I love every minute of it. I'll see you this afternoon."

After ending the call, I picked up a photo sitting on the counter next to me of Slater and I with Scottie - it was taken at the park before the twins were born. Slater and I had just picked Scottie up from his grandmother on Eve's side and brought him home to live with us after Eve's sudden passing. I traced my fingers over the picture. "Our family is complete. Scottie, I'm officially your mom, and you're my son. I love you, little boy." I wiped my misty eyes, still numb from the news. We'd been waiting for this day for months, and the emotions I felt were overwhelming and hard to control. My hands shook, tears flowed down my cheeks. "I need to call Slater and share this with him, I want to hear his voice," I whispered, picking up my phone.

# CHAPTER 2

## SLATER

*I* was feeling good about this job. Joseph Hansen, the real estate developer, liked my bids and the knowledge I'd shared with him from previous experience on other projects. He was younger than I expected - probably in his early forties, but that was definitely in my favor. During our two-hour meeting, along with Ricky, the conversation flowed easily, and we discovered we had quite a bit in common. He recently became the proud father of twin boys, and it turned out he didn't live too far away from me.

During our conversation, I mentioned that Sabela and I were in the market for a new house, having outgrown the condominium where we were currently living since the twins were born. He laughed at my remark and told me that he and his family had moved into a bigger home a few months before his boys were born. He said he may have some leads on houses and would give me a call later in the week. After our meeting ended, I leaned across his desk and gave him a firm handshake before standing.

"I want to go over my notes - I'll be in touch by the end of the week," Joseph said, as he stood and held out his hand to Ricky. "It was a pleasure to meet you too, Ricky. It sounds like you and Slater make a wonderful team."

Ricky shook his hand. "Thank you. It was an honor to meet you, too. Slater is a fantastic man to work for and has a great crew behind him. I can assure you that you won't be disappointed with our work."

Ricky patted my shoulder as we stood outside the elevator on the 12th floor of the office building, smiling. "I think that went rather well. What do you think?" he asked, smiling. "You seemed to have hit it off with him, and I was surprised how friendly he was. I was expecting some stiff in a suit and tie with no personality, someone that would look down on us. But man, he was the complete opposite - wearing jeans and a dress shirt, treating us like regular folk. He wasn't a snob at all."

I felt confident that I'd gotten the job and was certain my proud smile reflected it. "I think it went well, too. I like the guy, and I don't want to jinx it by saying I think we've got this," I laughed. "But honestly, I think we do," I said, patting Ricky on the back.

Walking through the underground parking lot to my truck, I pulled out my phone from my pocket, unmuted it and saw that I'd missed two calls from Sabela. "Shoot, Sabela called me twice. I hope everything is okay," I told Ricky before he got into the passenger side of my truck. "Let me call her real quick and then I'll drop you off at your place so you can pick up your truck and head over to the Richmond house to help the guys with the wooden floor installation."

Ricky nodded. "Sure, take your time."

Sabela answered the call straight away. "Sabela, is everything okay?"

"Yes, I figured you were still in your meeting. How did it go?"

"It went great. I'll know by the end of the week whether the job is ours, but I'm feeling rather good about it."

"That's great, honey! I'll keep my fingers crossed. I have some good news, too," Sabela chirped.

"What's that?" I asked.

"Claire called me this morning and our adoption papers arrived; we can pick them up today. Slater, it's official. I'm Scottie's legal mom. He has a new birth certificate and everything."

I froze, listening to Sabela as my knees became weak. Seeking support before I fell, I leaned against the truck. "Oh my god, Sabela, we need to celebrate!"

Sabela chuckled. "We will, but first we need to meet with Claire and pick up the documents. That's why I called - I want us all to go as a family. Let's go after we've picked Scottie up from school. What do you think?"

"I think that's a brilliant idea. I have a few hours of work to do, and then I can pick you and the girls up before I get Scottie."

"Perfect." Sabela paused: "Hey Slater, do you think Scottie understands how special this is?"

"I sure hope so, but maybe he's a little too young to feel the emotions we're experiencing. I think you'll always be Sabbie to him," Slater joked.

"Yeah, you're probably right, and I love the name Sabbie. He owns it! No one else calls me that. We can tell him that he can call me mom if he wants to, but I'm his Sabbie," Sabela giggled. "I'll see you this afternoon, love you."

"Love you too."

# CHAPTER 3

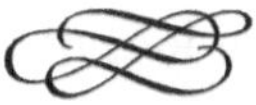

## SABELA

Slater returned home a few hours later as I was dressing Hope and Joy in matching yellow jumpsuits. Sometimes it was a challenge - both wanted to be picked up and fussed over at the same time, but it turns out Joy loves music, so as soon as I played a tune on my phone and set it in the crib next to her ear, she quickly stopped fussing and smiled as she wiggled to the beat of the music, giving me time to dress Hope.

I heard footsteps and looked over my shoulder while leaning over Hope's crib as Slater came into the room. "Hey, you're home," I said with a smile.

Slater approached me, wrapping his arms around my waist and resting his head on my shoulder. He smiled down at Hope whose big brown eyes lit up when she saw her daddy. "Hi, beautiful girl," Slater said, his eyes bright and full of love.

"Are you talking to me or Hope?" I joked. "The girls and I are almost ready; I just have to dress Joy and freshen up."

Slater kissed me on the cheek before pulling away, reaching into the crib to pick up Hope. "Daddy's missed you. Have you been a good girl?"

Hope gazed into her daddy's eyes and watched his lips as he spoke, touching them gently with her tiny fingers. My heart melted every time I watched them together. Sometimes I had to pinch myself, not believing what beautiful girls Slater and I had created. Watching Slater dance around the room with his daughter was something I'd never tire of seeing.

After Joy was dressed, my hair combed and make up applied, we took my new SUV that we had purchased shortly after the girls were born. I missed my old truck, but now that I was a mother of three, it was time to let it go.

 At the school Scottie greeted us with a huge grin, holding his latest masterpiece from his art class, telling us it was a sailboat on the ocean. I knelt before him and smiled, holding his creation. "That's beautiful, Scottie."

"Thanks, Sabbie." He looked up at his dad, love seeped from both their eyes. "Where are we going now, Daddy?"

Slater pushed the girl's double stroller back and forth as he spoke. "Well buddy, we have something special to do and it's about you."

Scottie creased his brow and curled his lip. "About me? What does that mean?"

We were interrupted by Scottie's teacher, Mrs. Eldridge, who greeted us with a smile before leaning in and giving each of the girls a tickle on the belly. "They're getting so big," she remarked, before making baby talk with Joy and Hope, who were mesmerized by the strange face invading their stroller.

"They certainly are," I agreed. "Before you know it, you'll be teaching them," I chuckled, taking Scottie's hand and giving him a huge grin. "And today we found out that I'm officially Scottie's mom. The final adoption papers came today, and we're picking them up after we leave here."

Mrs. Eldridge gasped and held her chest. "Oh, congratulations, that is such wonderful news! I know you've been waiting for this for such a long time." She took my hand and gave it a squeeze. "I'm so happy for all of you. Well, I don't want to keep you." She turned and looked at Scottie playing peekaboo with the twins. "I'll see you tomorrow, Scottie."

Without looking away from his sisters, he nodded. "Yes, Mrs. Eldridge."

Once we were all back in the SUV, the girls in their car seats with Scottie sitting in the middle on a booster seat, Slater drove so I could text Claire and let her know we were on our way.

"Where are we going, Daddy?" Scottie asked from the back seat.

I turned and gave Scottie a loving smile. "We're on our way to pick up some very important papers from Auntie Claire that say I'm officially your mommy, Scottie. Remember I told you that I was going to adopt you because I love you and Daddy?"

Scottie nodded. "Yeah, I remember."

"Well, the adoption is now final, and Claire has those papers that show I'm your mommy. It has your name, my name and daddy's name on it."

"What about Hope and Joy? Are they on it too?" Scottie asked.

Slater chuckled. "No son, they're your sisters; only Sabela is adopting you. Hope and Joy are already family, and now we're officially one big family, buddy. You can call Sabbie mommy if you want to."

Scottie looked at me with a creased brow. "I can? But she's Sabbie."

I reached over my seat and took Scottie's hand, "Yes buddy, I will always be Sabbie, but now you have a choice; if you decide you want to call me mommy sometimes you can."

"Nah, I like Sabbie," Scottie said, shaking his head.

Slater laughed and gave me a smirk, "I told you that you might be stuck with Sabbie."

I folded my arms and grinned. "No complaints from me."

When we arrived at the children's home, Open Arms, Travis

answered the door and greeted us with a friendly smile, shaking Slater's hand.

"Hey guys, come on in. Claire has been so excited for you both all day. You'd think it was her adopting," he laughed, closing the door behind us. Just then his phone rang. He pulled it out of his pocket and glanced at the screen. "Sorry guys, I need to take this. Our internet is down and they're supposed to be coming by this afternoon. I've been waiting all day," he said, shaking his head. "Why don't you make yourselves at home in the front room, I'll be back in minute," he said, going into the office to take his call.

We were greeted by Caroline, Travis' mom, who was in the adjoining kitchen pouring herself a glass of iced tea. She looked up and smiled. "Hey guys, how's it going? Claire is upstairs with her mom and Jill," she chuckled as she shook her head. "Jill is running some ideas by Claire to spruce up the girl's bathroom."

I rolled my eyes and laughed. "Please don't tell me it involves pink walls."

Caroline nodded. "Now that you mention it, I think I did hear the color pink."

I laughed again. "Quick, you have to go save Claire. If Jill had her way, the entire house would be pink."

Caroline took a sip of her tea and set the glass on the counter. "I'll let her know you're here. Have a seat in the front room, I'll be right back."

I nodded and welcomed the comfort of the couch as I set Hope, whom I had been holding, on the large area rug in front of the TV. Slater had the same thought and placed Joy next to her sister before joining me on the couch.

Scottie remained standing and tapped Slater's knee. "Dad, can I go play with my friends?"

"Sure buddy, they must all be upstairs."

Scottie sped off as he yelled, "okay, Dad!"

A few minutes later Claire joined us with her dog Tilly, a Yorkshire Terrier following close behind, greeting us with a huge smile.

She took my hand as she sat down next to me. "I'm so excited for you guys! The papers are in my office. Do you want me to go grab them?"

"In a few minutes. I want Scottie to be here, and he just took off to find his friends. Where is everybody, anyway?"

"Isn't it great how they all get along? The kids are always asking, when's Scottie coming over?" Claire laughed. "Everyone is upstairs, and Jill and I have been keeping them busy since classes ended."

I jumped at Tilly's sudden outburst as she barked at the double patio doors that led out onto the back lawn. I turned my head and laughed when I saw Maggie, Jill's Golden Retriever, on the other side of the door wagging her tail briskly.

"There's another two that have become inseparable. Jill brings Maggie to work every day and she keeps Tilly so busy! She's worn out by the end of the day and sleeps most of the night. I love it!" she laughed, opening the door for Tilly, giggling as she raced outside to be with her new best friend.

Claire glanced around the room. "Where did Travis go?"

"He's taking a phone call in the office," I told her.

Claire stood up and headed towards the kitchen. "Well, as soon as he comes out, we'll find Scottie and I'll grab the papers from the office. I can't wait much longer," she said, rubbing her hands together. "In the meantime, who wants some iced tea?"

# CHAPTER 4

## SABELA

*I* couldn't get over how good Claire looked dressed in loose-fitting turquoise pants and a matching cotton blouse. Even without make-up she was glowing, and her skin looked so healthy. "You look fantastic Claire," I told her, as she handed me a glass of iced tea and sat down next to me.

She smiled and rubbed her belly. "Thanks, other than sometimes feeling fatigued I'm doing extremely well."

"When are you due?"

"My doctor told me late June, or at the latest, early July. I had an ultrasound, and everything looks great. The baby's heartbeat is normal. We're just counting the days," she laughed.

I took a sip of my drink. "Do you know the sex of the baby?"

Claire shook her head. "Nope. Travis and I discussed it, and we don't want to know. We just want a healthy baby; the sex doesn't matter."

Slater nodded as he knelt on the floor between Hope and Joy, keeping them out of trouble by constantly pulling them back by their ankles when they scooted too far away.

Claire looked over at the twins and laughed as Slater held onto Hope's ankles. "Pretty soon they'll be crawling."

"Oh, any day now," Slater laughed, pulling Hope back next to his side.

I heard the door to the office close as Travis entered the room. "Sorry about that, but when your home is your business, there's no escaping it," he chuckled, placing his phone in his back pocket.

"You're not complaining, are you?" Slater asked with a hint of sarcasm, picking up Joy and handing her to me, and placing Hope in his lap.

Travis shook his head. "No, not at all man, I love every minute of this. The kids are amazing and they get along so well. It's just how we dreamt it would be; one big happy family."

Claire nodded in agreement. "I love waking up every morning and being greeted by six beautiful smiles. They really have come out of their shells."

"Even Jasmine? She's doing okay?" I interrupted.

"Yes, and as I mentioned on the phone earlier today, Jill has a lot to do with that. Jasmine really looks up to her. They go clothes shopping together, and Jill has even encouraged her to write in a journal. I think it's helping her a lot. It's the last thing Jasmine does every night before we turn the lights out. She likes to dress in her PJ's, take a cup of hot chocolate to bed, and get comfy under her blankets before writing in her journal."

"Have you read any of it?" I asked, bouncing Joy on my knee.

Claire shook her head. "No, Jill told her that she doesn't need to show it to any of us, only if she wants to. I think it's helped her to write more. If she were to show anyone her journal, I think it would be Jill."

I shook my head, knowing about Jasmine's past. "That poor girl. She's only seven and has been through so much. How long has she been in the system?"

"Five years, since she was two. Her parents were drug dealers and lost custody of her. When they were arrested, Jasmine was found in a closet screaming, bruises covering most of her body. From what I understand she doesn't remember much about it, but she's fearful of most people, which is understandable after what she's gone through. So, to see her warmup to Jill is a beautiful thing."

I nodded and smiled. "Jill does have a magnetic personality. You can't help but like her," I laughed. "We both know how difficult she can be at times, but we can never stay mad at her for long, right?"

Claire matched my laughter. "You're right about that. She has charisma that just draws you in. I can see why Jasmine has grown to trust her."

Joy began to fuss on my knee, and I turned to Slater. "Hey, did you bring in the diaper bag? We need to feed these two. Maybe they'll go down for a nap and we can get the adoption papers."

Slater stood up from the ottoman where he'd been entertaining Hope on his knee and faced Travis. "It's still in the car, I'll go grab it." He smiled at Travis. "Here, she's all yours for a minute."

I caught Claire smiling as she watched Travis rock Hope in his arms, humming her a tune. She released a heavy sigh. "He's such a natural with kids. You should see him at bedtime - every night all the children sit in a circle around him in one of the kids' rooms and he reads them a story. They look forward to it every night and pick whose room story time will be in. They all love him."

It warmed my heart to hear Claire's words. "Aww, that is wonderful. I knew you guys were the perfect fit for the children's home."

A few minutes later Slater returned with the diaper bag, set it on the floor at my feet and took Hope from Travis.

"Let me go grab the folding playpen. The twins can sleep in there," Travis said, leaving the room.

Claire held out her arms: "I'll take Joy from you Sabela, if you want to go make their bottles."

I took Claire up on her offer and headed for the kitchen where I made two bottles of formula, handing one to Slater.

"Do you want to feed Joy?" I asked Claire.

Claire smiled. "I'd love to."

I handed her the bottle. "While you're feeding the girls, I'm going to go look for Scottie."

I headed upstairs. After closing the safety gate, I found Jasmine and Jill in Jasmine's room. Jasmine was sitting in front of her mirror as Jill combed her mahogany brown curly hair. I tapped lightly on the open door and Jill turned her head.

"Hey Sabela, come in. I'm just fixing Jasmine's hair. We're going to take the dogs for a walk, do you want to join us?"

"I would love to, if Jasmine doesn't mind Scottie and I tagging along. It will give Slater a chance to catch up with Travis while the girls are asleep." I looked at Jasmine through the mirror. I didn't want to infringe or make her feel uncomfortable. "Is that okay with you, Jasmine?"

Jasmine looked at me through the mirror, her brown skin glowing from the lights around the mirror, and nodded without speaking.

"Okay, great. Can you give me about 15 minutes? I'm getting my official adoption papers for Scottie as soon as I find him," I laughed.

Jill's jaw dropped. "Oh, how exciting!" she squealed. "Yes! Take all the time you need."

"Where's everyone else?" I asked, looking around the room.

"They went down to the basement about ten minutes ago to watch a movie with Caroline and Claire's mom."

"Okay, thanks."

I found everyone in the spacious basement sprawled on the large L-shaped brown couch in front of the big flatscreen TV watching The Lion King. Scottie heard me walk in the room and turned his head. "Sabbie, come watch the movie with us."

"I'd love to buddy, but I'm here to take you upstairs so we could talk to Auntie Claire."

Scottie creased his brow. "Aww, but I want to stay and watch the movie."

"You can come back in a few minutes, unless you want to take the dogs for a walk with me and Jill."

Scottie jumped off the couch. "I want to take the doggies for a walk," he squealed.

I laughed at his enthusiasm and took his hand. "Come on, let's go upstairs first. Daddy and Claire are waiting for us."

Knowing the house like it was his second home, Scottie led the way, and I reminded him to be quiet before entering the front room. "Remember, the girls are probably sleeping by now, so we can't make a lot of noise."

"Okay, Sabbie," he replied, walking a few steps ahead of me.

Claire looked our way and smiled. "Oh good, you found him," she whispered so as not to wake the twins.

"Yes, he was downstairs watching a movie. Thanks for putting Joy down."

"Oh, no problem. I love the practice," she joked, giving both girls a caring smile as she peeked over the top of the playpen, pleased to see them sleeping soundly. She turned her head and gave me a big grin. "So, are we ready?"

Rubbing my hands together I nodded, looking over at Slater talking to Travis. "Are you ready, hon?"

Claire's eyes shined, her smile bright. "Okay everyone, have a seat and I'll be right back."

I took Scottie's hand and squeezed it tight as we made our way over to the couch and took a seat next to Slater. Scottie sat between us, and Slater reached behind Scottie's head and rested his hand on my shoulder. I reached up and took his hand.

Travis sat across the room, his arm resting on the arm of the couch, his legs straight out, crossed at the ankles. "Pretty exciting moment," he said, looking and smiling at Scottie.

Slater rubbed the top of Scottie's head. "It sure is, right buddy?"

Scottie twiddled his hands as he spoke. "I guess. Where did Auntie Claire go?" he asked, looking around the room.

"She went to go get the important papers I told you about earlier," Slater told him.

A few minutes later Claire returned, holding a brown file and wearing a huge smile. She stood before Slater and I and handed me the file. "Here they are," she said, still wearing a big smile.

I immediately felt a wave of emotions rush through me as I took the folder from Claire and laid it on my lap.

"Aren't you going to look at them?" Claire asked, her hands clasped together in front of her chest.

"Yes, I just need to compose myself. My hands are shaking, and my stomach is in knots right now. I've been waiting for this moment for so long, and now that it's here, it's overwhelming, emotionally. I didn't think it would affect me like this."

Slater squeezed my shoulder. "That's okay, take your time, sweetie. We've waited this long, what's a few more minutes?"

I stared at the folder and slowly picked it up.

"Come on Sabbie, open it. I want to go for a walk with Maggie and Tilly," Scottie said impatiently.

I chuckled and wiped a single tear that escaped my eye. "Okay, here goes." Slowly I opened the folder, and on top of all the other papers that had been filed during our pending case was a manila envelope. I lifted it out of the folder, my hands shaking slightly, and held it in my hand while setting the folder and other papers on the coffee table. I released a heavy sigh, smiled at Slater, and proceeded to open the envelope. I held my hand up to my mouth as I read the official adoption document, stating me as the mother and Scottie as my son. "Oh my goodness, it's real. I'm Scottie's mom!" I cried, handing the paper to Slater.

Slater read the document and smiled, his eyes misty. "You sure are, sweetheart." He looked at Scottie and leaned in, showing him the piece of paper with his name on it. "See buddy, there's your name and there's Sabbie's name. Isn't that cool? Sabbie is your mom."

Scottie looked at the paper and nodded. "That's cool, Daddy."

I leaned in and hugged Scottie. "I love you so much buddy," I said, tears streaming down my cheeks.

"I'm so happy for you guys," Claire said, wrapping her arms around Travis and leaning her head on his chest.

Travis kissed the top of Claire's head and held her close. "Yeah, this is pretty special. Someday, Scottie will realize just how lucky he is to have two amazing parents."

Slater patted Scottie's knee. "Thanks, Travis. I have to say, that's one thing Eve did do right, and that was to make sure I had custody of Scottie after her death. If she hadn't, I would never have known I had a son."

"And we wouldn't be sitting here giving you the adoption papers, and Open Arms would never have existed," Claire reminded us.

"You're right," Slater said, nodding. "We do owe Eve some thanks, even though she ran off with another guy," Slater said, shaking his head and letting out a slight chuckle. He raised his bottle of water and smiled. "To Eve, may you rest in peace."

I gave Slater a loving smile as we all raised our drinks. "To Eve!"

# CHAPTER 5

## SLATER

*I* wasn't expecting to toast Eve, but at that moment as I embraced my son and experiencing the joy of the completion of Sabela's adoption papers, I had come full circle and realized just how much I had Eve to thank for. She had her faults, scaring me when she left with no goodbyes or reason. I looked around the room in the grand mansion where we sat that was now the children's home, Open Arms, giving children a second chance, a new beginning in life. A home left to me by Eve after her tragic death with a short battle of brain cancer. I found out after her death through a letter she'd written me that I was Scottie's biological father. A son I never knew I had who came into mine and Sabela's life when he was four. I will be forever grateful to Eve for bringing us together and doing the right thing. I raised my glass again and smiled. "To family. Everyone in this room is family."

Sabela leaned over Scottie, smiled, and gave me a gentle kiss on the lips. "To family. I love you."

"I love you, too."

Scottie wriggled between us and stood up. "Can I go now? I want to go walk the dogs."

Sabela laughed and tickled his stomach. "Why don't you go upstairs and tell Jill we're ready."

Scottie didn't need to be told twice and raced out of the room, leaving us in laughter.

"I can't believe how big he's getting," Claire said, smiling. "And every day he looks more like you, Slater."

"He definitely has my hair before I cut mine."

"And your dark, mysterious brown eyes," Sabela added.

Sabela stood and peered into the playpen where the twins were still sleeping peacefully. "The girl's hair is beginning to come in a little bit; it looks like it might be dark. I wonder if they'll have thick, dark hair like their dad," Sabela said.

"I see both of you in them," Claire said, rubbing Travis' knee.

"Really?" Sabela said, looking closely at the girls.

"Yeah, they both have your chin Sabela, and your brown eyes. Slater has blue eyes."

"And what they both have is our time," I joked. "Alone time has been pretty scarce for Sabela and I. I'm looking forward to our honeymoon on Catalina Island." I smiled at Sabela and gave her a wink.

Sabela scooted next to me and took my hand. "I'm ready, too. I love our kids, but this woman here is yearning for some alone time with her husband."

"Well, what are you waiting for?" Claire asked, her brow creased. "You've been married almost three months now. We've been on ours, and so have Jill and Ricky."

I chuckled at Claire's remark and squeezed Sabela's hand. "We plan on going when the twins turn one."

Claire's jaw dropped. "That's six months away, guys. Do you think you can wait that long?" she laughed. "I knew you wanted to wait a little bit longer, but look at them, they're doing great."

Sabela interrupted. "I agree, they're doing wonderfully, but we wanted to make it as easy as possible on my mom and her boyfriend, Lorenzo. They'll be staying at our house watching all three of the kids while we're gone."

Claire leaned back on the couch and folded her arms. "Have you asked your mom if she wants to wait until the girls are older? Don't you think she could manage?"

I smirked at Claire. "No, we haven't asked Charlotte. We don't want it to be a burden on her."

Claire chuckled. "Slater, they're her granddaughters. I don't think they'll ever be a burden. I bet she's counting the days until they turn one so she can spend a full week with them, Scottie too." Claire smacked her knee and smiled. "I think you should go sooner. That's too long to wait. You guys haven't had a break since your wedding day. Your mom'll be fine; besides, you're forgetting that she can always call us if she has any problems. And that includes the rest of the gang - Jill, Ricky, Sadie and Logan."

I shook my head, "Claire, I can't just leave for a week. I just put in a bid for our first big job. I'm supposed to hear back by the end of the week. How would it look if I take off for Catalina for ten days?"

Claire wasn't fazed by her comments and persisted with her idea. "Slater, it's your business and you're the boss. When is the job supposed to start?"

"Well, not until next year - sometime in February, I believe."

Claire slapped her knee again. "There you go! What's stopping you from going now if the job doesn't start until next year?"

Sabela joined in on the conversation, "Claire, as much as I like your idea and would love to spend ten amazing days isolated on an island with Slater, it's the first week of November."

Claire laughed, "Sabela, we live in southern California. It's still gorgeous and warm here. I honestly think you should go," she insisted.

I pondered Claire's idea. She made a good argument, doing an excellent job of convincing me, and during our discussion it suddenly occurred to me that if I were to get the new construction job, I might not have a chance to escape in June once the job began. "What do you think, Sabela?"

Sabela narrowed her eyes. "You're seriously considering Claire's suggestion?"

"Well, I never thought of this before, but what if I get the condominium job: How can I leave in June during the middle of construction? That may not be possible."

"Oh wow, I never thought of that," Sabela agreed.

Claire clapped her hands. "See! There's another reason you should go sooner. Come on guys, you'll thank me when you get back," she said with a satisfying grin.

I chuckled. "Not so fast, Claire. You and Jill both had drama on your honeymoons. Knowing our luck, something's bound to happen."

Travis laughed. "Well, there's only one way to find out and that is to go. I agree with Claire, I think you should go; who knows when you'll be able to get away if you get the big job."

I looked at Sabela and shrugged my shoulders. "They're making some good points. What do you think? Do you want to push our honeymoon forward six months?"

Sabela smiled. "I think I do."

My eyes grew wide; her reply took me by surprise. "You do? Oh, wow!"

Claire stood and clapped her hands eagerly. "Yes, fantastic!"

Sabela raised her hands. "Hold on a second," she laughed. "This all depends on whether my mom can stay at our house for ten days on such short notice and watch the kids."

Claire waved her hands. "Like I said, she's their grandmother and she'll stop whatever she's doing in a heartbeat to be with her babies. That's what grandparents do."

I wrapped my arms around Sabela and pulled her in. "The more I think about your idea Claire, the more I love it, and honestly, it makes more sense to go now. I'm getting excited about the idea, and I honestly hope Charlotte and Lorenzo will say yes."

Sabela squeezed my thigh. "I love the idea too after talking about it. I am so ready to get away. I'll plead with my mom," she joked. "If I sense any kind of resistance, then I won't stop until she says yes." She patted my leg and stood up. "In the meantime, I promised Scottie we'd go for a walk with Jill, Jasmine and the dogs. Why don't I do that and then we can go home and call my mom."

"Great." I turned and gave Claire a smile. "Thanks, Claire. This was a damn clever idea you had."

Claire folded her arms, leaned back and smirked. "I know."

# CHAPTER 6

## SABELA

On our ride home from Claire's, I found myself sitting quietly in a daze, thinking about the possibility of going on a honeymoon within the next week. I must admit, Claire has a way with words, and her reasoning was something we couldn't challenge. When she first mentioned the idea I was totally against it, but now it seems to make a lot of sense, especially if Slater gets the big job. Slater was right, he'd probably never be able to get away once he starts.

Now I'm just hoping that my mom will agree to our sudden change of plans. My stomach churned, thinking she may have plans of her own and that I'd have to handle the disappointment. Claire pretty much pointed out that this could be our only chance to take our honeymoon for quite a while.

"You're pretty quiet," Slater said, keeping his eyes on the road.

"I'm sorry, I'm just stunned by how clever Claire was to convince us to change our honeymoon plans. That was pretty slick of her," I joked.

"But I agree with her one hundred percent." Slater turned and looked at me. "Do you?"

"I do, and now, I'm excited about it, but I'm worried that my mom won't be able to watch the kids. Then what? We have no one else we can ask to stay at the house."

"You're right. Well, we can't allow ourselves to get too excited until you've talked to your mom," Slater replied, patting my knee.

"Too late," I laughed. "Just the thought of being alone with you for ten days and ten nights, doing whatever we please whenever we want, excites the hell out of me." I turned and faced Slater, grabbing his arm and giving it a hard squeeze. "Do you realize that we'll be able to sleep in until noon if we want to?" I laughed and tossed my head back against the seat. "Hell, we could stay in bed all day if we decide to. When was the last time we stayed in bed past seven in the morning? That alone excites me." I suddenly had a terrifying thought. "What if we can't change our reservations at the Avalon Hotel? Do you think they'll let us switch on such short notice?"

"Gosh, I never thought of that. I'll call them as soon as we get home, and you can call your mom. We do have one thing in our favor," Slater said with a cute smile.

"What's that?" I asked, glancing in the back seat to check on the kids, happy to see they were all sleeping. I smiled, thinking the walk must have worn Scottie out.

"It's November and it won't be as busy as the peak months."

"You're right! I never thought about that." I leaned back in my seat and closed my eyes, thinking of sandy beaches, candlelit dinners and swimming in the ocean. "I sure hope Claire was right about the temperatures for this time of year on the island. I've never been, and I want to see and do as much as possible with you."

"I've never been either. We can also look up the forecast for next week tonight."

"I need to write a list. We suddenly have a lot to do," I said, suddenly feeling overwhelmed.

Slater patted my knee again. "No lists until we've made our

phone calls. If your mom says yes and we can change our reservations, then we start making a list. I also need to call Ricky and go over the schedule with him and let him know he'll be in charge. It's not a busy week and he should be just fine."

I nodded. "Good idea. I agree."

Scottie woke up as soon as Slater turned off the car in our driveway, sitting patiently in the middle of the back seat as Slater and I each grabbed a twin. The sun was setting quickly on the horizon, and I suddenly felt pressured about everything that needed to be done before I could even think about calling my mom. Dinner needed to be cooked, the twins needed to be bathed and fed, and Scottie needed to take a bath and eat dinner before settling down on the couch to watch an hour of TV before bed. This was our normal routine every night since the twins had been born. After the girls were asleep, Slater and I would manage to squeeze in an hour of cuddle time on the couch before we, too, began to fall asleep.

Scottie was in his PJ's by 8:00 pm and had settled on the couch after his bath and a frozen pizza, and the girls were sound asleep in their cribs in our room. A bedroom that we'd outgrown, but had no option than to share it with the girls, as the third bedroom was being used for an office. I was looking forward to house hunting soon and finding a home with at least four bedrooms to accommodate all of us.

After handing Scottie a juice box, I turned to Slater, sitting at the dining room table getting ready to call the Avalon Hotel. "Hey, can you call my phone? I can't find it," I said.

Slater chuckled. "How many times a day do I call your phone?"

"I know. I get so sidetracked with the girls, and I set it down wherever I am in the house." A few minutes later I heard the ringtone of my phone coming from the downstairs bathroom. "I hear it! Thank you. I'm going upstairs to call my mom, so you can call the hotel from down here and keep an eye on Scottie."

After retrieving my phone, I headed upstairs to the office,

closed the door behind me and let out a heavy sigh as I sat at the desk. Relieved to be able to finally sit down, I dialed my mom's number and hissed when her voicemail came on. "Damn it!"

'You've reached Charlotte. Please leave me a message and I'll get back to you as soon as I can. Thank you, and have a great day.'

"Hey Mom, it's Sabela; please call me as soon as you get this message. Love you, bye." I ended the call and leaned back in the chair, enjoying the peacefulness of being alone in the office. "I wonder where Mom is at this time of night?"

Disappointed that I hadn't been able to reach my mom on her land line or cell phone, I released a heavy sigh knowing our honeymoon lay in limbo until I did. Feeling frustrated, I grabbed my phone and headed back downstairs. Slater was still on the phone, so I took a seat across from him at the table and waited anxiously for the outcome of his call.

After a few minutes I sensed it was going well. He grabbed a notepad from the end of the table, recited a check in date for next week as well as a check out date, writing them down and looking at me with a satisfactory smile. I returned the smile, knowing he was changing our dates. Five minutes later he ended the call, leaned back in his chair, and rested his hands behind his head.

He smiled. "Well, that was easy. They said November is much slower and there's no problem changing our reservations. We check in this coming Monday." He paused. "I know it's only a few days away, but the week after they're booked up for a wedding, so I jumped on these dates. Hey, how'd it go with your mom?"

I frowned. "Not good, and now we're supposed to leave in three days."

Slater dropped his hands from behind his head and rested them on the table. "Oh no, don't tell me she can't watch the kids. I've already changed our reservations. I guess I should have waited until after you'd spoken to her."

"I still don't know if she can. She didn't answer her phone. I left her a message, asking her to call me back."

"Did you call the house phone or the cell phone?" Slater asked.

"I called both and she didn't answer either one. I don't even know why she has a cell phone. Half the time it's not on," I laughed.

"Why don't you try her cell phone again? If she's not home, she may have it on."

I picked up my phone, tried again and immediately hung up. "Nope, it went straight to voicemail."

"Damn it," Slater said, leaning back in his chair. "Well, there's nothing more we can do until she calls back."

"She'd better call back soon. We need an answer from her. I'm anxious to start packing. Shit! What if she says no?"

# CHAPTER 7

## SABELA

For the next hour, I kept picking up my phone, making sure it wasn't muted or that I hadn't missed a call from my mom, and whenever I walked around the house, I made sure I had my phone with me and not let it out of my sight.

"Nothing yet?" Slater asked, coming down the stairs after taking a shower.

I shook my head. "Nope. The one time I really need to talk to my mom and she's not home. Go figure."

Scottie was curled up next to me on the couch watching cartoons. I leaned in and kissed the top of his head. "Hey buddy, it's bedtime."

Scottie kicked his feet. "No, I wanna watch this," he whined.

Slater intervened and placed his hands on Scottie's knees, preventing him from moving his legs. "Hey buddy, what have I told you about talking back? You have school tomorrow. Now come on, Sabbie said it was bedtime." He held out his hand. "Let's go. I'll tuck you in."

Scottie threw his head back against the couch in a tantrum. "But I want to watch this. It's almost over."

Slater gave him a hard stare and took his hand. His voice was firm when he spoke. "Scottie, it's bedtime, now let's go," he insisted, pulling Scottie off the couch.

Scottie folded his arms and puckered his lips as he stormed across the living room. "Fine, but I'm not tired."

Slater chuckled. Just recently Scottie had been resisting bedtime, and Slater had to be the aggressive one, fighting the battle with him. He turned and smiled at me. "Here we go again. I'll be down in a minute."

I nodded. "Have fun," as I checked my phone again. Nothing. "Damn it Mom, will you please call me?" I mumbled to myself.

After making a cup of decaf coffee, I returned to the couch and changed the channel to a home decorating channel. Within minutes of putting up my feet and resting my head on a pillow, my phone rang. I jumped up and looked at the screen of my phone. I saw it was my mom. "Finally!" I said, picking up the phone.

"Mom, where have you been? I called you almost two hours ago."

"Lorenzo and I went out for dinner. We just got home. Is everything okay? And why the urgency, Sabela? Are the twins okay?"

A rush of guilt suddenly flooded me, realizing how abrupt and short my message had been that I'd left on her phone. "I'm so sorry Mom, everything's fine. I didn't mean to worry you."

"So, what's going on?"

I took a deep breath wishing I were speaking to her in person. "I know this is short notice Mom, and I will understand if you can't do it, but Slater and I have pushed up our honeymoon sooner and want to know if you'd still be able to watch the kids?"

"That's fabulous, I always thought you were waiting too long. When are you leaving?"

I hesitated. "In three days, but that's only if you're able to babysit."

"Wow! That is short notice. I was expecting you to say in two weeks or something," my mom said, unable to hide the surprise in her voice.

"I know Mom, but we went over to Claire's house this afternoon." I quickly changed the subject and became excited. "There's another thing I haven't told you yet - Scottie's final adoption papers arrived. We went to Claire's to pick them up." I smiled and held my chest. "I'm officially his mom."

My mom gasped. "Oh Sabela, that's wonderful! Is that why you've changed your honeymoon dates? Were you waiting for them?"

"No, Mom. It was Claire's idea, and it made a lot of sense. I don't know why we didn't think of it sooner. She made a good point when we told her that Slater had put in a bid for our first big contract which is supposed to start early next year. If he gets the job, he may not be able to take time off in June, which is when we were supposed to go on our honeymoon."

"Claire made a good point and I have to agree with her," my mom replied.

"So, what do you say, Mom? Can you watch the kids?" I asked, eagerly.

"Of course I can, sweetie. I'm retired now. My time is my own, and I know Lorenzo will love the idea, too. We'll start packing tomorrow."

I squealed into the phone. "Thank you, Mom. I love you. Why don't you come over on Sunday night, the day before we leave. We can spend the night together. I'll cook dinner and we can go over everything."

"Sounds great! Did you really think I'd say no? They're my grandbabies. What grandmother would say no to that?" my mom laughed.

I matched her laugh. "That's exactly what Claire said."

After ending the call, I released a huge sigh of relief and searched for a pad and pen to begin my list. After finding none downstairs, and anxious to put pen to paper, I raced upstairs to the office and found one on the desk. Without wasting a moment, I took a seat and began writing out my list.

Oblivious to my surroundings and writing with expediency trying to get my thoughts down quickly, Slater startled me as he entered the office. "Why are you working so late?" he asked, his brow furrowed.

I looked up and grinned. "I'm not working, I'm writing a list."

Slater walked over to where I sat and peered over my shoulder. "A list for what?"

I leaned back in my chair and gave him a huge smile. "A list for our honeymoon."

Slater's jaw dropped. "You talked to your mom and she said yes?"

I nodded; my smile still prominent. "Yep, she sure did. They'll be here Sunday night. I'll cook dinner and we can play games with the kids. Have a real family night, then go over everything before we leave Monday morning. I'm so excited."

Slater stood before me as I remained seated and leaned in, his hands resting on the arms of my chair. "I can't wait to get you alone," he whispered, kissing me tenderly on the lips. "Hmm, hurry up Monday."

I leaned forward and kissed him back. "The feeling is mutual."

# CHAPTER 8

## SLATER

Excited about our honeymoon, Sabela and I stayed up late researching Catalina Island online and all the fun things we could do.

"I want to do everything," Sabela said. "How are we going to do all these things in ten days? It's not enough time," she smirked. "Maybe we should go for a month," she said jokingly. She quickly jotted down items on her notepad each time she discovered a new activity. "I want to snorkel, rent an electric bike and go explore the island. I want to rent a dinghy and go fishing. Last time I went fishing was with my dad. I was just a kid," she laughed. Her eyes grew wide, "and, oh yes, I want to go kayaking, too!"

"We can rent a golf cart too," I added.

"I'm writing it down," she said excitedly and then returned to the computer screen. "Look, we can go on a glass bottom boat, too," she laughed, adding it to the list.

Lost in our world of discovery and excitement over our honeymoon, we stayed in the office until after 3:00 am and had huge regrets when Hope woke us three hours later at 6:00 am for her morning feeding. Soon after, her cries woke Joy.

"Oh my god, I feel like I just went to sleep," Sabela moaned, pulling a pillow over her head. "Hold on girls, we're coming."

I rubbed Sabela's naked stomach. "Why don't you lay here for a while, and I'll go make the girls bottles."

"You'll get no argument from me," Sabela said, removing the pillow and rubbing her eyes.

I returned with two warm bottles, finding Sabela dressed in her white bathrobe, holding Hope with one arm who was still fussing, while rubbing Joy's belly with the other, still in the crib. I handed her a bottle and picked up Joy.

Sabela yawned as she returned to the bed, Hope now curled in her arms and feeding. "I'm so tired. What were we thinking? I can't remember the last time we stayed up so late."

I sat on the other side of the bed feeding Joy and yawned. "I agree. Watch, we'll spend our entire honeymoon sleeping because we won't have these girls to wake us up," I laughed.

"Oh no we won't!" Sabela protested, followed by a high-pitched laugh. "Who knows when we'll be able to get away again after this. This might be our only chance for quite some time if you get the condo job."

A few minutes later, like clockwork, Scottie appeared in the doorway of our room, wearing his Scooby Doo PJ's and wiping his eyes. "I'm hungry," he whined.

"Okay buddy, as soon as we've fed the girls, I'll make you some breakfast. Why don't you go brush your teeth and comb your hair, then you can watch some cartoons."

"Okay," he replied, as he yawned again before heading toward the bathroom down the hall.

"So, what's on the agenda for today?" I asked Sabela as I fed Joy the last of her bottle.

Sabela stood up from the bed, Hope still cradled in her arms as she gently placed her in the crib. "We need to go shopping for our trip. We only have today because my mom and Lorenzo will be here tomorrow for dinner, and I need to clean the house and get things ready for them."

"Okay then, shopping it is," I confirmed. "I'll feed Scottie some breakfast and get him dressed while you deal with the girls, and we can be out of here within the hour."

"Sounds good to me. I'll see you downstairs in a bit, right after I've dressed myself and the girls."

The last thing I grabbed before getting in the car was my notepad. "You drive. I want to write a list on our way to the store," Sabela said, getting in on the passenger side.

I shook my head and laughed. "You and your lists."

"Well, I can't remember everything, and besides, I like checking things off," she said with a smug smile before turning her head and making sure the kids were all strapped in.

Once inside the store we grabbed two carts - one for the twins, who remained in their car seats, and one for the stuff we'd buy.

I took ahold of Scottie's hand and spoke to him in a firm voice. "Now, you stay close to us Scottie, don't go wandering off, we're not here to buy candy or toys. Understood?"

"I won't," Scottie replied, his hands on the side of the cart.

Sabela took the empty cart, and I pushed the cart with the twins in it as we headed over to the sales department.

"Look, they still have a lot of summer items on sale. We should find some great deals on sandals, shorts and even beach towels," Sabela said, smiling.

"I'm going to need some new tennis shoes and jeans," I told her.

"We can head over to the clothing department afterwards," she said, holding up a pair of yellow shorts and putting them in the cart.

After finding some good deals, we walked over to the men's clothing department. Sabela and I began digging through the jeans, looking for my size. "They have everything but my size and nothing's in order," I complained.

"Keep digging. People pick them up and never put them back in the right places. Their jeans are never organized, but I've always managed to find your size. It may take me a while, but I never give up," she laughed, picking up a pair, checking the size and then returning them to the shelf.

I was now on my knees, searching the bottom shelf. "I think we're out of luck; this is the last shelf," I told Sabela, now going through the shelves I'd already gone through.

"I already checked those."

"I know, but you didn't check all the way in the back, I was watching you." Suddenly she froze, a pair of jeans still in her hand. She scanned the area around us. "Where's Scottie?"

I quickly stood up and spun around, looking in all directions. "He was right here a minute ago," I said, my heart racing.

"Scottie!" Sabela yelled, throwing the jeans in her hand back on the shelf.

I echoed her words. "Scottie!" I shouted, my eyes darting in every space around us.

Sabela's eyes grew wide, gripped with fear. "Slater, he's not here."

My chest heaved as panic quickly set in. "Watch the girls," I yelled as I hastily began checking between the clothes hanging on the racks behind us. "Scottie! Where are you?" I yelled, pulling clothes aside on the racks and looking at the ground beneath them.

"No, I'm coming with you. He can't have gone too far," Sabela insisted, spinning the cart around with the girls. "Scottie, this isn't funny. Come on out wherever you are," she called, pushing the cart between the racks of clothes.

"Where the hell could he have gone? He was standing right next to me, I swear," I cried, my eyes darting in every direction, sweat building on my brow.

"We got so damn distracted looking for jeans, we weren't paying attention to him. God, where could he be?" Sabela cried, yelling his name again. "Scottie!"

I stopped an elderly couple, "Excuse me, have you seen a little boy with short, curly brown hair?" I held out my arm. "He's about this high."

The couple shook their heads and continued to walk past me.

"Okay, thank you."

A young lady approached the men's department; I stood in her path. "Excuse me, I'm looking for my son. He's almost six, have you seen him?"

She shook her head, "Sorry, no I haven't," she replied. I moved out of her way.

"Scottie, where the hell are you?" I whispered under my breath, my heart still pounding. I watched Sabela ask more people and my heart sank each time I saw them shake their heads.

I walked over to Sabela and took her hand, "come on, he's not here; let's start checking other parts of the store. I can't believe he took off like this after I told him to stay close."

Sabela turned the cart around with the girls and again shouted Scottie's name. "Scottie! Get over here now. We're not playing games."

I stood and scanned all the areas. "Come on Scottie, please come back," I begged, looking everywhere as we walked down the aisles. My heart continued to race, my palms drenched with sweat as I pushed the shopping cart. Horrific thoughts began to consume me. Did someone take him? I've heard of crazy, terrible stories of kids being abducted, never to be found. Please don't let this happen to Scottie, I pleaded silently.

I tried to backtrack in my mind when we were searching for jeans. How long did we spend looking for the right size? Was it two minutes, five minutes, maybe ten? How much time had passed since we'd realized Scottie was gone? I was living a parent's worst nightmare and I wanted it to end, now. Never again would I take my eyes off Scottie. Not even for a second. I had learnt my lesson and was now paying the price. God, I wish I could turn the clock back just fifteen minutes before this nightmare began.

Sabela walked ten paces ahead of me, her head turning in all directions, looking down every aisle, checking behind and in front of her. "We have to find him," she hollered, marching through the store, stopping and asking everyone that crossed her path. Each time I saw their heads shake, my heart sank further, and my fear now heightening.

"Come on Scottie, where the hell are you?" I said, a lump wedged in my throat, then I heard a laugh. It sounded like Scottie's and I quickened my pace to catch up with Sabela. "I swear I just heard his laugh," I said, panting.

Sabela stopped abruptly. "What? Are you sure?"

I nodded eagerly. "Yes, it was Scottie!" Again, I heard a little boy's laugh and my ears perked up. "Did you hear that?"

Sabela's eyes lit up. "Yes, I did. It came from the pet aisle." She quickly spun the cart around. "Come on, let's go!"

I took Sabela's hand, and together we raced down the main aisle and turned two aisles down into the pet aisle. My body suddenly drained itself of all the fear I'd been experiencing, replaced with relief. I raised my hand to my chest when I saw my son kneeling before a Golden Retriever wearing an orange vest, smothering him with kisses as he giggled. A middle-aged woman stood next to him, smiling.

"Oh my god, Scottie," I called, racing down the aisle ahead of Sabela.

Scottie turned and pulled his face away from the dog's wet tongue. "Daddy! Look, I made a new friend. She looks like Auntie Jill's dog, Maggie."

I pulled Scottie up into my arms and held him tight, never wanting to let him go. "Scottie, do you know how scared we've been? Don't ever take off like that, ever again. Do you hear me?" I looked at the woman, who had taken a step back, pulling her dog with her. I gave her a polite smile. "I'm so sorry, we've been looking for him frantically. I can't tell you how relieved I am; one minute he was there, the next he was gone."

Sabela reached us, panting, and tried to hush the girls who

were now fussing. She reached over and took Scottie's hand. "My god Scottie, you had us so worried."

The woman spoke. "It's okay. I asked him when he first came up to me and my dog where his mommy and daddy were, and he told me that you were looking at clothes and he got bored. I was under the impression you knew where he was."

I gave her a weak smile. "It's not your fault, please forgive me for my abruptness." I turned and gave Scottie a hard, stern stare. "My son should know better than to take off without telling us. I'm sure he saw your dog and began following you."

Scottie puckered his lip, tears filling his eyes. "I'm sorry Daddy, I just wanted to pet the doggie."

I pulled Scottie into my chest. "I know buddy, but you can't just take off like that. You must always stay close to me and Sabbie, okay? We thought something bad may have happened to you."

Scottie nodded, tears running down his cheeks. "Okay, Daddy. Can I pet the doggie again?"

I released my hold on him, set him on the ground and looked at the woman. "I'm Slater by the way, and this is my wife, Sabela." I smiled. "Can he pet your dog again?"

The woman returned the smile. "It's a pleasure to meet you; I'm Elaine, and this is my therapy dog, Enzo. She's my best friend and keeps me calm in busy places."

I reached down and pet Enzo alongside Scottie. "She sure is beautiful. She's got an unusual name. How did you come up with it?"

"I got the name from a great movie I watched called The Art of Racing in the Rain. I highly recommend it if you like dog movies. Anyway, the movie is about the life of a dog called Enzo. I loved the name, and even though the dog in the movie is a boy, I decided to give my baby girl the same name."

"I'll have to check it out," I replied, petting Enzo's head.

Scottie looked up. "Can we get one?" he pleaded. "I want a

Maggie dog." His eyes lit up. "If we get one, it can play with Maggie, too!"

I rubbed the top of his head. "Maybe after we get a bigger house we'll think about getting a dog, okay buddy?"

"Okay, Daddy."

After a few minutes of allowing Scottie to pet Enzo, the nice woman spoke. "Well, I really must get going. It was a pleasure meeting you both as well as your beautiful children. Have a wonderful day."

I shook her hand. "It was a pleasure meeting you, too."

After she'd left, I took Scottie's hand and gave it a little shake. "Now you, young man, are going to stay close to my side and not let go of my hand. Understood?"

Scottie shied away from my hard stare and my narrowed lips. "Yes, Daddy."

I turned and looked at Sabela who was trying to comfort the twins stirring in their car seats. "Let's make this quick, I am so done with shopping. I'll make do with the jeans I have at home," I said.

Sabela nodded, "I agree. I just need to get food for the week so that my mom doesn't have to go shopping. It won't take long. Let's go back and grab the other cart we abandoned by the jeans. Hopefully it's still there." She patted the girls' stomachs again. "These two will need to be fed soon as well."

I squeezed Scottie's hand. "If you let go of my hand buddy, you'll be in serious trouble. I never want to go through that, ever again," I told Scottie in a stern voice, hoping to instill some fear into him.

By the way he shied away and nodded in shame with his head hung low, I believe I succeeded.

# CHAPTER 9

## SABELA

After our horrendous shopping spree yesterday, we spent the afternoon at home lecturing Scottie about the seriousness of his actions and what could have been a much different outcome. We were upfront about the children that'd been kidnapped and taken away from their parents, never to be heard from again. We tried to explain to him that not everyone in the world is good, and that there were some bad people, the ones that we're trying to protect him from. It tore at my heart when he cried and threw himself into our arms, apologizing and telling us he'd never do it again. His tears told us we got through to him, and the fear in his eyes confirmed that.

My mom and Lorenzo arrived in the afternoon, a few minutes after I'd just flopped my body on the couch with a steaming hot cup of tea after spending the day cleaning and packing for our trip. I was finally done. The girls were down for their afternoon nap, and Scottie was playing Legos with Slater. I was exhausted and didn't realize how much work would be involved to escape on a ten-day trip, but we were excited and knew that all the effort we'd put into it would be worth it.

Slater answered the door while I remained on the couch savoring my tea. I turned and looked at my mom and immediately felt concerned. She looked pale and tired. I sat my cup on the coffee table, stood up and approached her. "Mom, are you okay?" I asked, hugging her.

"Yes, I'm just a little tired," she replied in a soft voice.

"Are you sure you're up to watching the kids? We don't have to go, Mom.

My mom waved her hand in protest. "You will do no such thing. We'll be fine. I just spent all day packing, and it took the wind out of me. Stop worrying, Sabela."

I wasn't buying it, and again brought up my concerns. "Mom, are you sure? You look so pale."

My mom gave me a weak smile, but I felt it wasn't genuine. Her eyes were telling me another story. She glanced away from my stare as she spoke. "Nothing a good night's sleep won't cure. Now will you please stop fussing and show Lorenzo where you want him to put our bags?"

For now, I granted my mom's wishes and stopped my interrogations, even though I wasn't convinced and had a sense she wasn't being honest with me.

I turned and looked at Lorenzo, standing by her holding two large black duffle bags. I held out my hand. "I'm sorry, hand me one of those bags Lorenzo, I'll put them in our room." I wasn't concerned about them sharing a room. Lorenzo had practically moved in with my mom since his mother also passed away shortly after our wedding. It brought me comfort knowing my mom wasn't living alone. They'd both lost their spouses which had brought them together in the first place, and were now giving each other support, as well as being there for one another. It was a beautiful relationship, and Lorenzo was now part of the family.

As we walked upstairs I said, "I've changed the sheets, but I'm afraid you'll be sharing the room with Hope and Joy. When we get back from our trip, house hunting is number one on our list," I laughed. "The girls are getting older and need their own room."

We entered the bedroom and I placed the duffle bag I was carrying on the bed; Lorenzo did the same. I paused for a moment, giving Lorenzo a concerned look. "Is my mom okay? She looks really tired."

Lorenzo released a nervous laugh. "Like your mama said, we are not getting any younger. We spent all day packing, and it wore her out. I am tired as well, but by tomorrow we will both be rested and fit as two fiddles," he said, laughing again.

I chuckled at his remark. "I'm sorry. I constantly worry about her since Dad died, and I need to stop. She has you, and you've been wonderful to her. Mom told me that you've retired, and that one of your sons is now running the bakery - how do you like being retired?"

"Well, I get to spend more time with Charlotte, your mama, and my son is doing a fantastic job running the bakery. I knew he would; he is just like me, his Papa and my Papa." He raised his hand, pressing two fingers against his lips, and kissed them like the proud Italian that he was. "Grandpapa, he taught me everything I know; and now, I am teaching my boy."

I smiled and folded my arms. "I'm so happy my mom and I walked into your bakery that day in search of a wedding cake. My wedding brought you two together, and I'm so glad you found each other." I hesitated and smiled. "Do you think you two will ever get married?"

Lorenzo's smile suddenly disappeared, and I felt that I'd made him uncomfortable. Guilt quickly took over. I reached out and touched his arm. "I'm so sorry, I didn't mean to pry. It's really none of my business."

He patted my hand resting on his arm. "No, it is okay. Your Mama and I have never discussed it. We enjoy each other's company, and we are happy the way it is." He raised his hand and gave his chin a gentle rub. "Do you not like me living with your mama because we are not married, Sabela?" Lorenzo asked, his brow furrowed.

I felt my cheeks turn a shade of red, wishing I'd never pried. "If you're happy, I'm happy, and that's all that matters," I smiled. "Come on, let's go downstairs. I have chicken in the oven with all the fixings."

"Sabela, what time are you leaving tomorrow?" my mom asked, as we sat around the dining room table after a delicious meal, our bellies full and in a food coma, fatigue setting in.

I looked over at Slater sitting next to me. "The ferry leaves out of Dana Point at noon, right?" I asked him.

Slater nodded. "Yes, we need to check in an hour before, so we have to leave here no later than 9:30 am. Traffic may be heavy, so I'd like to have plenty of time to get there."

Over dinner we'd gone over everything with Lorenzo and my mom. I checked my list, pleased to see that I hadn't left anything out. It was a lengthy list, but this was the first time they'd be watching all three kids by themselves for over a week, and I wanted to make sure I'd covered everything from Scottie's routine in the mornings before school to the twin's feeding schedules, as well as their likes and dislikes. I made sure they had emergency numbers, which included our closest circle of friends, and a release note for emergency medical care. To say I was nervous was an understatement.

After checking off the last item on my list, I smiled and put down my pen. "I don't think I've forgotten anything, do you, Mom?"

My mom chuckled from across the table, leaning into Scottie who sat between her and Lorenzo. "Don't you worry about a thing. We're going to have so much fun, aren't we, Scottie?" she said, tickling him on the arm. He giggled and nodded, trying to resist the tickle. "You're two hours away by boat and car, Sabela, and you can call me every day. Don't you worry about a thing. You and

Slater are long overdue for some alone time," my mom reassured me.

I gave my mom a caring smile. "Thanks Mom, we're looking forward to it, but please, call us if you need us to come home early for any reason. We'll be on the next ferry home, I promise."

Slater stood and began clearing the table. He looked over at Scottie. "Come on buddy, help me with the dishes and then you can watch a movie with Grandma and Lorenzo before going to bed."

"I'll help you put the girls down," my mom offered, standing up to go check on the twins playing in the playpen.

"That'd be great Mom, thanks. You guys get our bed tonight, too."

"And where are you and Slater going to sleep?" my mom asked.

"Our couches fold out to full-size beds," I said, smiling.

After everyone had gone to bed and the house was finally quiet, Slater and I pulled out the hide-a-bed in the couch, and together we laid down the sheets, quilt and pillows before changing into PJ's (something I wasn't used to wearing) and crawled under the covers.

I cuddled up close to Slater and rested my head on his chest, enjoying the gentle beating of his heart in my ear, my arm draped around his waist, which I gently squeezed as I released a big sigh.

"Are you okay?" Slater asked, concerned.

"Yeah, I just hope my mom and Lorenzo will be okay. She looked really tired tonight."

Slater kissed the top of my head and squeezed my shoulder, pulling me in closer. "Babe, you worry too much. They've already told you that they spent all day packing and it wore them out. They're fine. They just need some rest."

"I hope you're right." I patted his chest, "let's get some sleep. I love you."

"I love you, too," Slater whispered, turning off the lamp.

# CHAPTER 10

## SLATER

*I* was awakened by Scottie jumping on my stomach, and my body tensed up from the sudden weight pressing down on me. I laughed as I tickled him ferociously. "Hey buddy, who needs an alarm clock when I have you?!" I gave him a bear hug and kissed the top of his head before pulling myself up to a sitting position. Then I noticed that Sabela's side was empty. "Where's Sabbie?" I asked Scottie, who was sitting on the edge of the fold-out bed next to me.

"Her and Grandma are feeding Hope and Joy."

I pulled myself off the bed and stretched. "Come on buddy, let's fix you some breakfast and get you ready for school. Grandma and Lorenzo are taking you so that Sabbie and I can get ready for our trip."

By 9:00 am we had everything in the SUV. Charlotte and Lorenzo had returned from taking Scottie to school, and the twins were playing with plastic blocks in the playpen in the living room.

"Okay Mom, are you sure you're going to be okay?" Sabela asked, as she put on a grey jacket.

Charlotte rolled her eyes. "Sabela, how many times do I have to tell you? We have everything under control. Quit worrying and go have the honeymoon that you two deserve."

Sabela embraced her mom and gave her a peck on the cheek. "Promise me that you'll call if you need us to come home for any reason. I don't care how trivial you think it is."

"I promise. Now get out of here," her mom said, nudging her arm on Sabela's.

Once in the car, I set the GPS on the dash and headed for the #5 freeway towards Dana Point. Sabela leaned back in her seat and released a satisfactory sigh. "Freedom!" she laughed. "I can't believe that for the next ten days it'll just be you and me!"

I reached across and rubbed her thigh. "Believe it, baby. The next ten days are going to be pure bliss." I gave her a smirk. "And before you start worrying about the kids, they'll be just fine. Your mom is over the moon about spending over a week with them."

"I know they'll be fine, and I was relieved to see that Mom looked much better this morning. I noticed the color had returned to her cheeks; like she said, it was just fatigue."

I was glad that we'd left early. It gave us extra time to get to the Catalina Express Terminal. Traffic was backed up due to an accident which was nothing new; traveling anywhere on the freeways in southern California was basically the same. The terminal was busy, with lots of passengers standing in line with their luggage waiting to check in.

"Why don't I go grab us some coffee and a muffin while you stand in line," Sabela suggested. "I'm starving. I only had time for a cup of coffee this morning before leaving the house."

"Sounds good, there's a line at the food vendor, too," I said, pointing.

Within the hour we were boarding the ferry, which resembled the inside of an airplane on water. All the seats faced one way, and were in rows with three aisles. We were lucky enough to get two seats next to a window, and behind us at the back of the middle aisle was a snack bar. We traveled light, just two bags, and were able to bring them onboard with us to our seats instead of storing them in the cargo area.

"I'm surprised to see this many people going to the island on a weekday, and in the middle of November," I told Sabela as we took our seats.

"Well, we both know it's a popular place year-round, and look at the weather; blue skies and warm temperatures. It still feels like summer."

"True. At least it's not as busy as the summertime months. There's still a lot of empty seats," I pointed out.

A few minutes later, the crew closed the doors to the vessel and the engines were fired up. I looked out the window and saw one of the crew members untie the line from the dock and jump on the deck as we pulled away.

"We're off!" Sabela said excitedly, squeezing my knee.

I took her hand, raised it to my lips and kissed it. "We sure are, baby. We're finally going to celebrate our honeymoon in style."

The crossing to Catalina would only take an hour. After enjoying the view of the vast ocean from our seats, I suggested to Sabela that we go stand on deck at the stern of and watch the view of the mainland disappear in the distance.

She didn't hesitate as she looked into my eyes, smiled, and immediately stood up. "Good idea."

I was glad the ocean was somewhat flat and the swells small, as I still needed to find my balance as we walked to the stern of the boat, holding on to available rails and the backs of seats as I walked by. The salty breeze blowing in from the open door hit me before I stepped outside and took in the magnificent view of the massive ocean. The fresh air filled my lungs. I breathed in deeply as I took hold of the brass rail, and holding Sabela's hand, I guided her next to me where she, too, took hold of the rail. I wrapped my arm around her waist and pulled her in. Her long, dark hair blew chaotically in all directions.

I leaned over and looked into the water. I was mesmerized by the ferry cutting through the ocean, creating waves and crests of whitewater. "God, this feels good," I hollered to Sabela over the loud engines.

"It sure does," Sabela shouted into my ear.

We stood amongst a dozen other passengers enjoying the ride, reminding ourselves we were experiencing a sense of freedom from the bustling cities that we'd dealt with every day. Within 30 minutes, the skyline of the mainland could no longer be seen. I leaned my head closer to Sabela's ear. "Do you want to walk up to the bow and see if we can see the island?"

Sabela smiled and nodded. "Yes. Let's go."

When we reached the bow, there was more room to move around, and we quickly spotted two open seats, taking ownership immediately.

"I see it!" Sabela squealed. "Wow, it's gorgeous," she added, grinning at the spectacular view before us.

"Man, why haven't we come here sooner? Look at those white condos on the hillside overlooking the ocean - what an amazing place to live!"

We were still about 15 minutes from Avalon Harbor, but the island was in clear sight with its rugged, natural terrain and magnificent dominance. I spotted sail and power boats cruising along the coastline, some anchored; I assumed they were fishing. Suddenly the crowd around us became restless, pointing out to sea and cheering. I looked in the direction where everyone was looking and gasped. "Sabela, look - dolphins!"

Sabela quickly stood up. "Where?" and immediately started to jump up and down like a child when she spotted them. "Oh my goodness, look at them, Slater! I've never seen such a sight. It's like they're welcoming us to Catalina."

I looked out to sea and grinned as I watched the pod of dolphins swim close to the boat, following it and jumping through the waves, arching their bodies perfectly as they reentered the water. "Wow! That's awesome," I yelled, mesmerized by the beauty of nature before me.

"That was amazing," Sabela said, taking my hand as we returned to our seats, grabbing the bags we'd stuffed under our seats.

When we stepped off the boat onto the dock and walked up the ramp, I stopped and stared out at the beautiful harbor filled with boats of all sizes glistening beneath the sun and gently rocking in the harbor, anchored at their mooring.

"Wow! Will you look at this place? It's incredible, and so peaceful," I said, taking it all in.

Sabela stood next to me wearing a huge smile. "This is breathtaking." She pointed to a large, beautiful, ornate round, white building with a red-tiled roof across the harbor. "That's the casino and theatre we saw online."

"Yes, it is. We'll have to check it out while we're here. I think the tours are still going on."

I looked up and down the wide path where we stood. Passengers were still walking up the ramp. To our left were gift shops, restrooms, and the ferry building. The other direction led to the heart of Avalon lined with more gift shops, bike rentals, kayak and dinghy rentals, and a few restaurants with tables and chairs outside lining the pathways. I looked up at the hillsides and admired the mansions and Mediterranean-style homes nestled amongst the trees and greenery with a million-dollar view of the luscious harbor. "Wow! Can you imagine living here? Look at those houses," I gasped.

Sabela stopped walking and admired the view. "This place is amazing!" she squealed.

I took Sabela's hand. "Come on, let's get checked into the hotel, then we can start exploring."

Sabela gave me a loving smile. "I want to explore you," she laughed, leaning in and giving me a passionate kiss on the lips.

"Alone in a hotel room with you. We're not leaving for a while," she said, kissing me again.

I wrapped my arms around her waist and pulled her in, returning the fiery kiss. "If we don't get to the hotel soon, I'm going to seduce you right here," I laughed, kissing her once more.

"No complaints from me," Sabela laughed, tossing back her head, allowing her mane of long hair to flow freely down her back.

# CHAPTER 11

## SABELA

We reached the hotel within ten minutes, avoiding the temptation to stop at every store and browse. We had one thing on our minds - to be alone in a room with no interruptions and make passionate love with one another. I was turned on by the thought, and my skin tingled with excitement.

Just a few blocks from the main street, the hotel overlooked the harbor, and like most of the buildings on the island, had the relaxing Mediterranean décor and feel. Standing at the front desk, I stood close to Slater, my arm wrapped around his waist and my head leaning on his shoulder as Slater checked us in. Breathing in his scent, I raised my head and gave him butterfly kisses on his neck as he spoke to the young lady behind the desk. I whispered in his ear: "Hurry up. I want you."

He turned, smiled, and whispered as the friendly receptionist looked up our reservations on the computer. "I want you too, babe."

Five minutes later we were standing outside our room, anxious to enter. Slater slid the room card into the lock and opened the door when the light turned green. I followed him into the room and grinned. "Wow, this place is gorgeous!"

Natural sunlight shined through the double French doors that led out to a balcony overlooking the harbor with two wooden deck chairs and a small, blue-tiled tabletop. I opened the doors and held my head up to the gentle breeze that tickled my face.

"God, that fresh air feels and smells so good," I said, spinning around with my arms spread wide.

The room was spacious, decorated with nautical pictures and aqua and pastel-colored walls. I was pleased to see there was a full-size bathtub.

Slater set down our bags on the nearby white leather couch and took me in his arms. "It's just you and me, babe." He glanced around the room and smiled. "Listen to that. The beauty of silence," he chuckled.

I kissed him on the lips and pulled him in. "I want you to make love to me," I said with a luring smile as I stepped back, removed my jacket and tossed it on the couch. Slater took a step forward, kissed me, and looked down at my heaving chest. Slowly he began to undress me, gently unbuttoning my shirt, kissing my neck, and rolling his tongue across my now exposed black lace bra. "You smell so good," he whispered, pulling my shirt free of my arms. My skin tingled from his touch, and the hairs on the back of my neck tickled, ignited by the passion and lust between us. Standing before him with my eyes closed and my head light, I melted to the touch of his hands caressing my breast as well as the warmth of his lips kissing my abdomen. I rested my hands on his shoulders to balance myself as he continued to kiss my stomach and unbutton my jeans, then gently pull down the zipper.

"Let's lie down on the bed," he whispered. "I want to lose myself in you."

I sat on the edge of the bed in my black bra and jeans and laid back. Slater stood before me, then knelt on the floor and proceeded to slowly peel my jeans off and free my body.

"God, you're magnificent," he said, his chest heaving.

Within seconds, he smothered his body with mine and kissed me passionately. Tangled together in a fiery fervor, our arms and legs wrapped around each other's bodies, we continued to explore each other's mouths with our tongues. Smothering one another with our scents, rolling our now joined bodies around the bed, staying sealed as one with a hungry kiss, hunting with our tongues and never letting go. We rolled together until I was on top, our lips still locked. Slater unclipped my bra and slipped the straps down my arms, freeing my breasts. We kissed long and hard as our hearts beat quickly, our brows sweat, and our skin on fire with desire. Our moans were heavy and long. Our gasps were strong as we became entangled with lust, finally having the freedom to be as loud as we wanted and expressing our desires for one another. Either of us held anything back.

We were hungry for each other at a level we'd not experienced since becoming parents. We released months of passion and lust that'd been restricted by parenthood. The lovemaking was raw, deep and passionate, and we both came several times. After each climax, our hearts raced, our chests heaved, and we let a few minutes go by to catch our breath before losing ourselves in each other again. After the third orgasm, we flopped our heads on the pillows - my hair damp, and my body trembling and moist from the passion I'd just released.

I raised my hand up to my brow while my chest continued to heave as I sucked in air. "Wow! That was months of suppressed lovemaking that we just let go," I laughed.

Slater's breaths were as heavy as mine. "No kidding! We need to come here every weekend just for this," he joked. He pulled me into his arms as I rested my head on his chest.

"I love you so much, Slater," I said, my eyes closed. "We have a great life, don't we?"

He kissed the top of my head. "I love you too, Sabela. We do have a good life, and if I get that contract for the condos, it'll be a game changer for us. I'll finally be working with the big guys, and it can only lead to more of the same deals and better things."

"This could be huge for us. I wonder when you'll find out if you have the contract or not?"

"He said it would be within the week, so I'm keeping my phone with me at all times," Slater said, reaching over and picking up his phone from the end table, then setting it back down.

We lay in each other's arms for the next ten minutes. Slater's heartbeat had finally returned to normal with the beating of it soothing my ear. The gentle breeze blowing through the French doors swirled the light as well as the white, sheer curtains into a dance. I was in heaven. I released a contented sigh before I pulled myself away from the embrace of Slater and reached for my phone.

"I need to call my mom and let her know we arrived okay. I also want to know how everything is at home." I stood up and walked over to the bathroom where I found two luxurious white bathrobes hanging on hooks. I grabbed them and threw one on the bed next to Slater and wrapped myself in the other one. "Want to join me outside on the deck?"

Slater sat up and slid his body into the bathrobe. "Sure," he replied, tying the belt around his waist.

I sat in one of the oversized cushioned blue and white chairs on the spacious deck and breathed in the salty, fresh air. "This place is incredible. I can't believe we've never been here before. It's only an hour away by boat."

The view we had was spectacular, overlooking the harbor and the small, sandy beach. There wasn't a cloud in the sky, and the temperature was in the seventies. "It's November, and the weather's gorgeous. The temperature is perfect," I said, closing my eyes and resting my head on the back of the chair.

Slater leaned back in his chair. "And it's not too busy, either. Seems like this is the perfect time of year to come here. I've heard it gets pretty crowded in the peak summer months." He turned his head, looked at me and smiled. "Could you imagine living here and waking up to this every morning? It would be like you're on vacation every day."

I released a heavy sigh. "Oh, one can only dream. I feel so far away from society here, and it's hard to believe that a place like this exists just an hour from the mainland."

"You know something else I've noticed?" Slater said, sitting up and looking over at the main street paralleling the ocean and the beach area, lined with restaurants and gift shops.

I looked where his eyes were focused. "No, what's that?"

"There're no cars. Everyone is driving golf carts."

I looked down at the streets. "You're right. I never noticed that until you pointed it out. That's another reason why it's so quiet here."

Slater glanced up and down the roads again. "I don't see one car. I love that. God, this place keeps getting better and better." He stood up. "Why don't I go see what drinks are in the wet bar while you call your mom?"

I nodded. "Good idea, and then afterwards we can get dressed and go explore."

Slater left the balcony as I picked up my phone from the table next to me and called my mom. It was a little after one and I assumed she'd be home with the girls while Scottie was in school. I'd given her specific instructions to keep her cell phone charged and answer it if it rang. After calling her number and hearing a few rings I was afraid she hadn't listened to me, until the sound of Lorenzo's voice took me by surprise.

"Hello," he said in his thick, Italian accent.

"Hi Lorenzo, it's Sabela. I'm just calling to let you know we arrived okay, and it's beautiful here. Where's my mom?"

I sensed the hesitation in his voice before he replied. "She is laying down. She has a headache."

I failed to hide the worry in my voice. "Is she okay? And what about the girls, are they okay?"

"The girls are fine, they make me laugh all the time. Your bambinos are growing up so fast. Before you know it they will be walking. I put them on the carpet in the front room and they are into everything. They can scooch their little bodies very quickly. I think they will be crawling any day now," Lorenzo laughed.

I laughed at his comments. "Yes, they do move quickly. You can put them in the playpen when you've had enough of chasing them," I told him.

"Oh, they are in there now. Your mama is fine. Don't you worry, okay? She is getting up in a little bit so we can go pick Scottie up from school. Everything is fine here. You and Slater have a fun time and we will talk to you tomorrow. Okay?"

Chills ran through my body as I listened to Lorenzo. His voice sounded unsettling, and I sensed he was trying to rush me off the phone. I've never known my mom to take a nap in the middle of the day. "Lorenzo, are you sure Mom's okay?" I asked. "We can catch the next boat back to the mainland and be home in a few hours."

"You will do no such thing," Lorenzo barked, catching me off guard. "You are on your honeymoon. I will have your mom call you after we have picked up Scottie. Will that make you feel better? You can talk to her yourself and see that she is fine."

"I'm sorry, Lorenzo. I'm already missing the girls and Scottie. We've never been away from them for even one night. Yes, have Mom call me this afternoon."

After I'd ended the call, worry still consumed me as I sat quietly on the balcony lost in my thoughts. Was I overreacting? Is this how parents act when they're away from their children, especially for the first time? Do they worry about everything? We've only been gone a few hours, and my mother is laying down. The twins are a handful and by the end of the day I know I'm exhausted. Maybe watching them for over a week would be too much for them. My concerns elevated when I began to think of the busy daily routines Slater and I have raising our three kids. It wasn't easy, and we're half their age. I suddenly found myself having doubts about whether my mom and Lorenzo would be able to manage the kids for that length of time. What was I thinking?

Slater startled me when he returned to the balcony holding two cold bottles of beer and two glasses. "Look what I found," he said, smiling and taking a seat next to me. His smile soon disappeared when he saw the worried look on my face. "Are you okay?"

"I just got off the phone with Lorenzo and he said my mom was lying down."

"She's tired. Those kids can be a handful," he joked.

I sat up and raked my hand though my hair. "That's just it. My mom has never taken naps during the day. Maybe watching the kids is too much for her. Do you think they'll be okay?"

Slater took a sip of his beer after pouring it into a glass and reached for my hand. "I'm sure they'll be fine. So your mom took a nap. Lorenzo is there too, and it sounds like they have everything under control." He squeezed my hand. "There's two of them, and yes, they're older than us, so of course it might be a little more tiring for them. But don't worry, okay? And don't forget, Jill and Claire said they'd go by during the week and check on them. I'm sure they'll take the girls to the park too, to give your mom and Lorenzo a break. They'd mentioned that."

I nodded and took a sip of my beer. "I'm sure you're right, but she's my mom, and I just can't help but worry."

Slater raised his hand and rubbed my shoulder. "You have every right to worry. It's natural, but don't let it consume you, because then you won't have a good time." He gave my shoulder a little shake. "It's our honeymoon, and we're going to have a great time, okay?"

"Yeah. I'm sorry. I'll quit worrying." I took a sip of my beer. "Let's drink up and go explore."

Slater smiled. "That's my girl."

# CHAPTER 12

## SLATER

Sabela soon snapped out of her worried thoughts, and after getting dressed, we spent the rest of the afternoon exploring the island. We decided to take a walk first out on the pier, and found a place to rent kayaks.

"Oh, let's do that tomorrow!" Sabela said excitedly. "I've never been in a kayak," she confessed.

"Me neither. I've spent all my time surfing, but I've never tried kayaking. This trip is going to introduce us to all kinds of new hobbies. After breakfast tomorrow we can rent a double kayak for a few hours, and then maybe lay out on the beach. What do you say?"

"Yes, and then maybe do some snorkeling in the afternoon?" Sabela said, grinning from ear-to-ear.

"Sounds perfect to me." I took her in my arms and kissed her passionately on the lips. "I could get used to this. Spending days with just you, doing whatever we want."

Sabela laughed, tossing back her head. "Well, don't get too used to it. Next week we become parents again."

I continued to hold her in my arms, gazing into her beautiful brown eyes. "We'll have to bring the kids here; Scottie would love it. There's so much to do, and I want him to love the ocean like we do." I looked around at the spectacular views. "God, this would be a great place to raise our kids."

"Yeah, but you gotta be able to make a living, too. I don't see a lot of construction going on here," Sabela noted.

I released my embrace and took her hand. "I can dream, can't I?" I said with a smirk. "Come on, let's rent a golf cart and go explore. Afterwards I'll take you out to a nice fancy restaurant for dinner."

Sabela leaned in and kissed me. "I love your plan."

"You know what I love about this place?" I said, as we left the pier, holding hands and walking over to the golf cart rental building.

"No, what's that?" she asked, swinging our entwined hands as we walked.

"Everything is within walking distance. There's no need for a car here. Imagine the money you'd save on gas," I stated, my eyes wide.

The guy at the golf cart rental building told us that very few people owned cars, most of them had golf carts. To bring a car onto the island was expensive and banned for tourists.

"Wow! A life without cars - can you imagine?" I said, as we stepped into our golf cart and drove off. It was my first time driving one, and I laughed at the lack of power it had going up the many hills and windy roads cut into the edge of the hillsides, but it also made sense. Even for this time of year, there were many pedestrians walking in the roads.

"Can you believe it's November?" Sabela said, leaning back in her seat wearing sunglasses and admiring the view of the harbor from the high road we were on. "I mean, check this out -  it's seventy degrees and it feels like summertime."

"I know. I'm kinda of glad we came here sooner and didn't wait until June of next year. I bet you there'll be four times as many people then."

"Me too," Sabela agreed, pulling her wind-blown hair away from her face.

At the higher altitude of the road, we stopped at the designated turnout overlooking the harbor and the small quaint town of Avalon, taking in the view. I was in awe. The more time I spent on this island, the more I fell in love with it.

Two white mansions at the top of the hill before the road descended back into town caught our attention. We stopped and peered at the massive homes and ornate, luscious grounds through the large heavy metal gates.

"Wow! Can you imagine living here?" I said, my eyes bright. "I wonder how much this place costs?"

Sabela chuckled. "More than we'll ever make. Come on, let's go. Our hour rental is almost up."

Driving back into town we took some of the side roads behind the main street. Clusters of little cottages painted in nautical blue, white and aqua colors lined the streets. We took Falls Canyon Road away from the homes and stopped when we came upon a pasture of green grass and a school.

"This is the Avalon school," I told Sabela. "I read about it online. It's the only school on the island, and all the kids from K-12 attend."

Sabela creased her brow. "Really? I wonder if the high school kids get to work with the young ones. I love that idea: Teach the older generation to respect and look out for the younger ones."

"It's a small school. God, this would be a great school for Scottie and the girls when they get older," I said, smiling.

Sabela laughed and patted my chest. "There you go, dreaming again."

I gave her a smirk. "Hey, there's nothing wrong with dreaming, but you have to admit, there's no better place to raise kids." I spun around, my arms spread like an eagle. "I mean look at this place, it's amazing!"

Sabela took my hand and led me back to the golf cart. "Come on, let's go return this thing and find a place to eat. I'm getting hungry."

I reluctantly started up the golf cart and drove past the school, admiring the grounds surrounding it, the playground areas and sporting fields, and the small size of the place. The whole time I was picturing Scottie in all of those areas. We drove around the bend and through the upper streets, where we passed some larger homes with nice yards and plenty of shade trees. One caught my attention, and I stopped the golf cart.

"What are you doing?" Sabela asked, her brow furrowed.

I stepped out of the cart and walked towards the sign in front of the house. "This one is for sale," I said, grabbing a flyer from the box underneath the sign.

Sabela shook her head. "Slater, we can't afford anything on this island."

I walked back to the cart while reading the flyer, ignoring Sabela's statement. "This one has four bedrooms and two bathrooms."

"And it costs how much?" Sabela asked, her arms folded across her chest.

I scanned the flyer for the price and frowned. "Two point five million."

Sabela's jaw dropped. "Ouch!"

Disappointment immediately set in. "Yeah, I guess you're right, we'll never afford a place like this," I replied, folding the flyer and putting it in the back pocket of my jeans, but I wasn't letting go of the dream just yet. My head was spinning with dreams of raising my family here and living life to the fullest. I've traveled a lot up and down California doing construction, and I've never been to a better place. No, my dreams had just begun, now what could I do to make them become a reality?

# CHAPTER 13

## SABELA

Over dinner at a seafood restaurant overlooking the harbor, Slater pulled out the flyer of the house for sale. He opened it and began reading off the description. "This would be the perfect house for our family, Sabela," he said with a loving smile.

I shook my head and chuckled, "Slater, we can't live here."

"Why not? It has everything we need; it's quiet, safe for the kids and you can't find a better view. I mean Sabela, think about it. This would be our backyard - the ocean, beaches, miles of trails through the hillsides. Everything we ever wanted to do is right here. Boating, swimming, kayaking, scuba diving, snorkeling and hiking. I could go on; the list is endless."

I couldn't believe he was considering living on the island. One thing I have learned about Slater over the years is that when he sets his mind on something, he goes with it and becomes obsessed. I had to bring him back down to earth. "Slater, you can't be serious? We have too many commitments back home. We can't just pack it all in and move here. And besides, there's no way we could afford it, and what if you get that huge job building condos? Are you going to take the ferry to work every day? And how would you get to the job site without a truck?"

"I haven't thought out all the details yet Sabela, but I'm really drawn to this place. You can't tell me that you don't like it, too. I mean, compared to where we live now in a three-bedroom condo, in a housing track with nothing but homes and shopping centers for miles, and Scottie's school has four times as many kids as the one here which is for all grades, what's not to like about this place?" he paused. "And I'll tell you something else, if I do get the contract for the condos, it will change our lives drastically. And, with some of Eve's money, which by the way would technically be going to giving Scottie a good home, I think we could actually pull this off."

I listened to Slater as he tried his best to convince me to jump on board with his crazy idea and dreams. It all sounded so good the way he described it, and yes, it would be perfect for our family, but I wasn't ready to take such a giant leap and leave everything behind. I still didn't know how Slater would manage working on the mainland while living on the island.

I shrugged my shoulders, "Oh, I don't know Slater. This idea of yours has come out of nowhere and I'm feeling overwhelmed right now. Our plan has always been to buy a lovely home with a big yard for the kids in the suburbs. We were going to start looking when we got back home. Now you suddenly want to move to an island in the middle of the Pacific Ocean away from everything; our friends, my mom, Lorenzo and a stable living. It's a little much for me to take in over dinner."

Slater continued to persuade me. "It's only an hour away, Sabela, but what's cool about this place, it feels like we're hundreds of miles away from civilization, when really, we're not." Slater reached across the table and took my hand. "Sweetheart, I don't want to pressure you into anything you don't want to do. We've always talked about everything, and I'm simply sharing with you how much I've fallen in love with this place and what dreams it's stirred up. But tell me one thing." He paused. "Could you see your-self living here if we were able to?"

I hesitated before answering. "Slater, this is a beautiful place. Like you said, it would feel like we're on vacation every day and it would be amazing to raise our kids here, but I'm a realist, whereas you are the dreamer in the family," I chuckled. "I can't get my hopes up and take a big fall when we come to realize that living here is simply out of our reach."

Slater grinned and squeezed my hand. "Never say never. I'm not going to say any more about it. Let's finish our meal. How about we take a nice stroll on the beach and watch the sun go down before we go back to our room and I have my way with you."

I giggled. "That sounds like the perfect plan to me. Especially the last part."

# CHAPTER 14

## SLATER

After an intense night of lovemaking, I woke up with Sabela naked and wrapped in my arms. The sweet scent of her hair made me smile, and I couldn't help but feel like the luckiest man in the world. I had a beautiful wife, three amazing kids, good friends that were like family, and a successful business.

I glanced out at the French doors where the sun peered in and thought how incredible it would be to wake up here every morning. Sabela stirred in my arms, and I gently kissed the top of her head. "Hey sleeping beauty, it's a new day," I whispered softly.

Sabela stirred again before rubbing her eyes. "What time is it?"

I leaned in and pulled her close. "Time for me to give you a kiss," I whispered, touching her lips with mine in a sensual manner before exploring her mouth with my tongue. "God, you're so beautiful in the morning," I said, kissing her ravenously, using my entire mouth to cover hers and French kiss her deeply.

Sabela wrapped her arms around my neck and matched the passion of my kiss. Even after three hours of non-stop caressing, as well as all the lovemaking last night, we were hungry for more this morning. Sabela reached down between my legs and took my now erect manhood into her hands, caressing it with long strokes as she continued to kiss me hard. "Make love to me. I want to feel you inside of me," she whispered.

I rolled over until I was on top of her, remaining locked with her lips. Sabela arched her back and spread her legs as she guided my hard shaft into her. We moaned together as we became one, our bodies sliding against one another as I explored every inch of her, thrusting my hips and riding her to climax. Her orgasm was strong and intense and her moans loud as her body stiffened and she cried out in ecstasy. I continued to ride her, increasing my speed, thrusting harder and quicker until I could no longer hold back.

Within minutes, I yelled her name as I came inside of her, my head spinning and my heart racing from the powerful climax. When I was finished, I rolled off of her, my heart still pounding, my breathing heavy. I rested my hand on my brow as I allowed my heart rate to return to normal.

"Wow! I want to wake up like this every morning," I joked.

Sabela giggled and pulled the white cotton sheet over her body. "Tell the twins that, who like to wake us up before the sun rises," she replied, resting her head on my chest and an arm around my waist. "I could lay here all day in your arms. This is heaven," she said, her eyes closed.

I gave her body a squeeze. "There's nothing to say we can't. It's just you and me for the next nine days. If you want to spend the entire day in bed, then that's what we'll do."

Sabela raised her head and looked out of the French doors. "Look how sunny it is. I love how the morning sun shines through the doors. This is definitely a piece of heaven." She patted my chest before sitting up. "Let's get some breakfast and take a stroll on the beach. I bet the water is warm enough to take a dip, too," she suggested.

Before I had a chance to reply, my phone rang on the nightstand. I glanced at the screen. "Oh shit! It's Joseph Hansen, the real estate developer."

Sabela's jaw dropped. "Oh crap. Take the call. I'm going to go sit out on the balcony so you can have some peace and quiet." She smiled. "I hope it's good news."

Sabela quickly pulled on a white bathrobe draped over one of the chairs and left the room. Once I was alone, I answered the call. My nerves peaked as I spoke. "Good morning, Joseph."

"Slater, I hope I'm not calling you too early."

"No, not at all," I replied, trying to sound calm, even though I was sweating bullets.

"Wonderful. I was anxious to call and not keep you waiting any longer. I've decided to hire you and your company for my project. I hope you're still able to take the job?"

My jaw dropped and my body became tense from the news. I wanted to scream aloud at the top of my lungs and let the entire world know how much this news meant to me and how much it would change my life.

Joseph spoke again. "Slater, did you hear me?"

I shook my head, realizing I hadn't answered. "Oh, I'm sorry. Yes, I heard you, thank you so much. I can't tell you how much this means to me and how excited I am to work with you."

"Fantastic. I'd like to schedule a meeting so we can go over the contracts and plans. When would be a suitable time? I'd like to take care of this as soon as possible."

I hesitated, wondering if I should confess that I wouldn't be available all week. "Right now, I'm on Catalina Island on my honeymoon. We'll be back next week. Any day after that would be fine."

"Oh for heaven's sakes, why didn't you say so? Next week'll be fine. Call me when you're back in town and we'll get together. In the meantime, I'm going to get off the phone so you can go enjoy your honeymoon with your wife. I won't keep you any longer."

"I'll call you as soon as we're home. Again, thank you so much."

"No need to thank me, Slater. You're an impressive young man and seem to know your stuff. I think this will go quite well. I look forward to meeting with you next week."

"Thank you, me too."

I was numb. After hanging up the phone, I sat on the edge of the bed in a daze. I couldn't believe I had the job. All the years I've spent hustling and getting side jobs, increasing my knowledge at each new job, and finally getting my contractor's license and running my own company has led me up to this moment. It was all beginning to pay off. I was working in the big leagues now, and it would only get better. This was opening doors to what I hope will be endless opportunities.

I suddenly remembered Sabela sitting out on the balcony, probably anxiously awaiting the outcome of the call. I quickly stood up and grabbed the other bathrobe on the leather couch, tossed it on, and still tying the belt around my waist, I joined Sabela on the deck.

The morning sun glistened in her hair. She looked radiant, wearing shades and sipping on a bottle of water. She looked up with a worried expression. "So, how did it go?"

As soon as my face broke out into a smile, she grinned. "You got it?"

My smile increased to a huge grin. "I sure did! We got the job, baby."

Sabela squealed as she quickly stood up and raced into my arms. "Oh my goodness! I don't believe it!"

I took her in my arms and spun her around before kissing her hard on the lips. "I know! I'm in shock, I can't believe it either. He wants me to call him when we get back home and schedule a meeting." I quickly broke our embrace. "Oh, shit! I need to call Ricky and tell him the news. I'm sure he's dying to know, and I want him to go to the meeting with me."

Sabela patted my chest. "Yes! You need to tell him. I'm going to get dressed while you do that, then we can celebrate with a fancy breakfast and go hang out on the beach for a while."

I leaned in and gave her another kiss. "Sounds good to me. My phone's on the bed, I'll make it quick."

Twenty minutes later, after telling Ricky the good news, Sabela appeared from the bathroom wearing denim shorts and a white t-shirt, her hair tied back in a ponytail. "Man, you are so beautiful," I smiled.

Sabela grabbed a lightweight backpack from the couch and began placing items that we'd need in it. "How'd it go with Ricky?"

"He's in shock, just like me. I told him that he'll be getting a raise; I think I made his day," I chuckled.

Sabela continued to place things into the backpack - two light-weight towels, suntan lotion and her phone. She turned and looked at me. "Come on, get dressed, I'm almost ready to go."

I pulled my hands out of the pockets of my bathrobe. "Give me five minutes," I said, as I walked by and gave her a peck on the cheek. "What a terrific way to start the day. Lovemaking with my wife, and a phone call letting me know I've been hired for a high-paying position. Nothing can ruin this day," I said, smiling and feeling good.

# CHAPTER 15

## SABELA

Life had certainly taken a turn for the better. I was so happy and proud for Slater; he had worked so hard for this moment. He shined over breakfast, smiling with his bright eyes, talking about our future, and how he would give me and the kids the best life possible. Then he surprised me.

He reached across the table and took hold of my hand. "I want to go see that house that's for sale. Let's call a real estate agent."

I released a nervous giggle. "Slater, are you still dreaming about moving here?"

"It doesn't have to be a dream, Sabela. This job changes everything. We could actually make this happen."

I shook my head. "Slater, we don't even know how much you'll be making, and I honestly don't think it will be enough to buy a three-million-dollar home. We just don't have that kind of money, babe."

"Maybe you're right, but I just want to take a look at it. What harm can it do?"

I leaned back in my chair. "But why? It will only crush you even more when you see it and know you can't have it. Why torment yourself like that?"

"Never say never. I guess I'm curious what a three-million-dollar home looks like on the inside." I gave her hand a squeeze. "Come on babe, if you insist that nothing will come of it, what are you worried about? Let's just take a look and be done with my crazy dream, as you call it."

Hoping that this would put an end to his ridiculous idea and that he'd soon realize that he was dreaming too big, I agreed to his crazy idea. "Okay then, let's go. We can go there first before going to the beach. Why don't you make the call to the real estate office, and then we'll rent a golf cart. I'm not walking up that hill," I laughed.

Sally, from the real estate agent's office, agreed to meet us at the house in an hour. After finishing our omelets, we rented a golf cart and arrived at the house ten minutes early. The tall, wooden fence to the property had a padlock on it, but I was able to peek over the beige-painted concrete wall as Slater stood next to me and did the same.

"It has a lot of yard space which is shaded with palm trees. And I like that it's all fenced in and on a quiet street away from town," Slater said. Then added, "this would be a great space for the kids to play in." He looked up and down the street. "And look, there's no cars on the entire island."

I continued to peer over the fence. It was a great yard - much bigger than I'd imagined, with a patio area off of the two French doors which I assumed led to a dining area. There was an expensive, stainless-steel barbecue, a wooden patio table that seated six, and two lounge chairs. "It is a nice yard," I agreed. "But we can't afford this, Slater."

Slater took my hand and gave it a little squeeze. "I just want to take a look. I didn't say we were buying it," he reassured me.

I folded my arms. "Well, good. Because we can't," I said sternly.

A few minutes later, a red golf cart pulled up behind us and a middle-aged woman with blonde hair wearing shades and a matching white skirt and top waved to us.

I assumed it was Sally, and smiled and waved back as Slater walked over and shook her hand.

"I hope you haven't been waiting long," she said with a friendly smile, stepping out of the golf cart.

"No, we just got here," Slater replied. "This place is amazing," Slater said, excitedly following her to the gate.

"Wait till you see the inside," Sally said with a big smile as she unlocked the gate with a code.

"How long has it been on the market?" Slater asked, following her into the yard.

Sally continued to walk through the yard to the front door as she spoke. "Three days. It won't be on the market for long. Property never is here on the island. It's usually snapped up fairly quickly. If you're serious about this place, I wouldn't wait too long," she said, unlocking the door and holding it open to allow us to walk in.

My jaw dropped when I stepped inside the glistening white foyer of the house and stood on the white tiled floor. "This is gorgeous," I gasped as I looked over at the large white framed mirror and then up at the white fan above.

"The entire house has tiled floors, white walls and furnishings. It keeps the house cool during the summer months," Sally told us as she led us to a large kitchen, complete with an island, white granite counter tops, top-of-the-line stainless steel appliances and white cupboards.

"This kitchen is huge!" Slater said, taking my hand. "We could all fit in here and cook as a family," he pointed out.

I nodded, "Yes, we could. It's a very nice kitchen."

"Let me show you the rest of the house," Sally said, leaving the kitchen and walking into the adjoining dining room where I saw the two French doors that led out into the yard where we'd walked through.

"How many bedrooms are there?" Slater asked.

"There are four bedrooms and two baths," Sally replied. "Let me show you where they are."

We spent the next thirty minutes touring the house. Our favorite spot was the veranda off the main living room, which overlooked the entire town with a magnificent view of the ocean and harbor. "I could sit out here all day," I said, admiring the view and enjoying the heat of the sun.

"Yes, this is a great area," Sally replied. "This side of the house gets most of the sun which is nice, and the yard stays shaded and cool most of the time because of all of the trees," she explained.

"Thank you so much for showing us the house," Slater said as we followed Sally to the front door.

"You're welcome, and as I said, if you're interested, don't wait too long. It won't be on the market very much longer. In fact, I'm showing it tomorrow morning to a couple who are arriving on the morning ferry."

"Oh wow! I guess buying property on the island is pretty competitive?" Slater asked, closing the door behind him.

Sally made sure the door was locked. "Yes, it's because the market is limited. Not a lot of houses go up for sale here, so when they do, it tends to be a bidding war and they sell quickly. I wouldn't be surprised if this one sells for above the asking price."

Slater's eyes grew wide. "Really? Oh wow! Then if that's the case, we definitely won't be able to afford this."

I was relieved when Slater finally came down to earth and admitted that the house was one we couldn't afford, but the disappointment in his eyes and the disappearance of his smile pained me.

I took Slater's hand and gave him a caring smile. "It was nice to check it out, though."

He forced a smile and nodded.

I turned to Sally. "Thank you so much for showing it to us."

She released a professional smile. "My pleasure. Don't hesitate to call me if you have any questions or would like to place an offer."

Slater gave a sarcastic smirk. "Oh, I can't see that happening, but thank you anyway. We'll let you lock up." He shook her hand. "It was nice to meet you."

Slater and I walked back to the golf cart in silence, his hands in the front pockets of his jeans and his head hung low, looking at the ground. I hated seeing him this way. The dream he'd been carrying for the last few days was no longer, and I knew he was hurting.

Once seated in the golf cart I gave his thigh a gentle rub and leaned into him. "Hey, we'll find a nice home. There's many more out there."

He didn't look at me when he spoke and fired up the golf cart. "Yeah, but they aren't on this island. Seems like there's very few homes for sale here, according to Sally. There's a few two bedroom condos, but they're smaller than what we're living in now, and I don't want to live in another condo." He finally managed to show me a weak smile. "I'm sorry, babe. I've just fallen in love with this place, and I've done nothing but dream about raising our kids here in a beautiful home overlooking the ocean since I first stepped off the boat. It's just so perfect, and realizing that it's just that - a dream - and like you said something we'd never be able to afford, kinda knocked the wind out of me."

My heart sank, listening to him. When he first mentioned moving here, I went along with it, thinking how cute he was being and that it was fun to dream. There's no harm in that, but I misunderstood - it was more than a dream; his heart was set on actually moving here, and now he was crushed. "Slater, I'm so sorry. We will find the perfect home for our family, and we can bring the kids here every summer and make many fond memories for them. That would be great, wouldn't it? Summers here, every year?"

Slater smiled again which lifted my heart. "Yeah, we could do that, I suppose. I just want them to experience this place and what it has to offer, like we are. I'm just blown away by it."

"I am, too. I had no idea a place like this even existed. I've heard of Catalina Island, but I wasn't expecting this." I changed the subject. "Speaking of which, what do you say that we go and enjoy more of it and check out the beach. It's even warm enough to lay out and maybe even go for a dip in the ocean."

"Sounds like a great idea. After all, we are on our honeymoon; I need to snap out of this depressing mood." He leaned in and kissed me. "I love you."

# CHAPTER 16

## SLATER

Sabela was right. Heck, she's always right. When am I going to learn to listen to her more often? I'm not going to lie; I'm disappointed that my dream that's consumed me since we first stepped foot on this amazing island may never come true. I finally realized it after talking to Sally, the real estate agent. I had no idea how scarce and expensive property was here. A tiny condo is over eight hundred thousand dollars. That's insane. What do people do for a living to be able afford to live here I wondered? I'm going to be making what I thought was a decent salary, but obviously not enough to live here. I just want what's best for my family, and this place seems to have it all.

Before starting the golf cart, I gave the house one last look. It stung knowing it'd never be ours, it would've been perfect. I released a heavy sigh and gave Sabela a forced smile. "Ready?"

She nodded and gave me a caring smile. "Yeah, let's get out of here and enjoy the rest of our day," she said, patting my knee.

"You got it." I paused and placed my hand on her thigh. "And I'm sorry for going overboard with my dream, I guess I got a little carried away."

Her smile grew. "It's okay, honey. It was a wonderful dream; I was almost sold on it."

I chuckled. "It was, but a little too big." I started the golf cart and pulled away from the curb. It was a short, five-minute ride back into the main part of town. That was another thing I loved about this place, the size. The entire town is under three square miles. Everything is within walking distance, and beyond the town are miles of hiking trails into the wilderness.

After returning the golf cart to the rental store, we walked through town to our hotel and grabbed some towels. Then we stopped at a nearby café across from the beach and got coffee and muffins to go. Wedging both towels under her arm, Sabela carried the muffins and skipped across the street to the sandy beach waterfront. I carefully followed her carrying two cups of hot coffee. I stood on the sand as Sabela laid out our towels, patting the empty one next to her once she'd sat down with the bag of muffins between us. Before joining her, I handed her a cup and took a sip of mine. I glanced up and down at the small beach. "Can you believe it's November?"

Sabela laughed. "No, it feels like summertime."

The water was crystal blue, the air was still, and the beach was relatively quiet. I assumed it was because it was a weekday and the kids were in school.

Sabela kicked off her sandals and dug her toes into the sand. "Hmm, it's been a while since we've done this. Let's spend the entire day here and maybe go rent a kayak later?" She turned and grinned. "Wouldn't that be fun? Then we can have lunch at one of those restaurants on Main Street."

I smiled and laid back on the towel, resting my arm behind my head. "Sounds great!" I closed my eyes, enjoying the morning sun. As I was about to drift off, Sabela nudged my side with her elbow. "Hey, let's get our feet wet."

I opened my eyes and shaded them from the sun with my hand

as I looked at her. "You didn't bring your bathing suit. If we're going for lunch, you don't want to get your shorts wet."

"I didn't say swim, I just want to walk out up to my knees and feel the cool water on my skin." She released a heavy sigh. "I haven't been in the ocean for a while, and it looks so inviting." She patted my chest. "You know what? You stay right here. You look so relaxed, and I know that you were almost asleep when I nudged you."

"Are you sure? You're right, I was dozing off, and laying here sure feels good." I rubbed my brow. "I can't believe I'm sweating." I gave her a hard stare. "Are you sure you don't mind?"

"Not at all. I'll just be a minute and then I'll lay down with you."

"Okay, I'll wait right here for you. Have fun," I replied, smiling.

I lifted my head, shading my eyes from the sun, admiring Sabela's beauty as she trotted off down to the water, thinking what a lucky man I was. Once she'd reached the edge of the water, I laid my head back down and closed my eyes, drifting off to sleep.

The next thing I remember was hearing an ear-piercing scream; I wasn't sure if I was dreaming until I heard the scream again, followed by my name being called.

"Slater! Help me!"

I immediately sat up, my heart racing, not knowing what had happened; then I heard Sabela scream my name again.

"Slater!"

Oh my god, what the hell is happening? I stood up and panic grabbed ahold of me, my body trembling with fear. I spotted Sabela on her hands and knees crawling in the shallow water trying to get to the beach. "I'm coming!" I yelled, racing towards her. In seconds I was at her side, knee-deep in water as her face disappeared beneath the surface. "Sabela!" I screamed, placing my two hands under her armpits and dragging her to shore.

She coughed in between her agonizing screams of pain, spitting out saltwater from her mouth. "Oh my god it hurts! Make it stop!" she screamed, as I continued to drag her to safety.

"What hurts? Sabela! What happened?" I shouted, my voice filled with fear. When we got to the sand, her body collapsed and she continued to scream.

"Something bit me in the water. It hurts so much," she cried, tears streaming down her face.

Suddenly a middle-aged man with shoulder-length blonde hair wearing beige shorts and a matching short-sleeved shirt appeared out of nowhere. "Come on, I'll help you get her up to the dry sand," he said, leaning down to help me.

Unsure of where he came from, riddled with fear and unsure of what to do, I nodded and took Sabela's ankles as he lifted her up underneath her arms.

"Thank you," I said, my voice shaking. "She's been bitten by something, but I'm not sure where."

Sabela continued to scream in pain as we carried her up to our towels. A small crowd of onlookers and concerned people followed us. We carefully laid Sabela on the towel, her ear-piercing screams tearing at my heart. "Where'd you get bitten?" I asked, trying to pull her hair away from her face.

Sabela lifted her leg. "My foot. It bit the underside of my foot. The pain is unbearable. Please make it stop!" she screamed.

The stranger who'd helped out took the empty towel, rolling it up and placing it under Sabela's head.

"I don't think she was bitten, I think she was stung by a bat ray," he said, positioning Sabela's head on the towel.

My brow furrowed, "a what?" I said.

"A bat ray. They live in the sand out here, but if you happen to step on one and startle it, they'll get you with their stinger. She wasn't bit, she was stung," he informed me.

Suddenly Sabela's body stiffened, and she held her throat. "I can't breathe. My god, what's happening? I'm so dizzy." Her body shook as I watched in horror as she began to spasm.

"Sabela! Sabela, can you hear me?" I said in a panicked state.

"She's going into anaphylactic shock. She must be allergic to the poison that was left by the stinger," the stranger said. "Do you happen to have an EpiPen?" he asked me. "It will reverse the allergic reaction," he told me.

I shook my head vigorously. "No! She's not allergic to anything; why would we have one of those?"

Sabela's body continued to spasm, her pupils disappearing into her eyelids, showing only the white part of her eyes. I was petrified and felt so helpless.

"Her pulse is dropping. We need to call an ambulance and get her to a hospital now! Where's your phone?" the man said urgently.

Without letting go of Sabela, I reached into my back pocket and pulled out my phone. "Please hurry," I begged, handing him the phone.

# CHAPTER 17

## SLATER

*I* continued to rest my hand on Sabela's stomach, trying to steady her body as it continued to convulse as the man whose name I still didn't know called for help.

He ended the call less than a minute later. "The ambulance is on its way. We need to make sure she doesn't go into cardiac arrest; she's having a severe reaction."

Within seconds I heard the sirens. Another advantage of this small island - when you call for an ambulance, it's here within minutes. "Hang in there, Sabela. An ambulance is on its way," I said, my voice shaking.

As I tried to comfort Sabela in any way that I could, a middle-aged redheaded woman wearing denim shorts and a white tank top joined us.

"What's going on?" she asked.

The man took her hand as she knelt beside him. "This is my wife Tammy, and I'm Dwayne." He looked at his wife. "I think she's been stung by a bat ray and has gone into anaphylactic shock," he told her.

Tammy gasped. "Oh, no! I hear the ambulance; they should be here any minute."

Sabela was struggling to breathe and kept fading in and out of consciousness. "Stay with me, Sabela," I said desperately, shaking her body gently. I looked down at her foot where she'd been stung and saw that it'd swelled up like a balloon. "Look at her foot. Jesus!"

Dwayne looked over at the street next to the beach where a crowd of people had gathered. "I see the ambulance. I'm going to go meet them and flag them down." He turned to his wife Tammy. "Sit next to her and hold her head steady," he said before leaving.

Tammy nodded and knelt next to Sabela. I gave her a weak smile. "Thank you for helping us."

Tammy gave me a kindhearted smile as she rested her hand on one of Sabela's shoulders. "She'll be okay."

I closed my eyes to hold back the tears. "I hope you're right. She's my world, and our kids can't lose their mother." I managed to give her a warm smile. "We just had twin girls six months ago, Hope and Joy. They look just like their mother."

Tammy touched my hand which was resting on Sabela's stomach. "That's wonderful. Congratulations."

Within minutes the ambulance pulled up alongside the beach. Spectators quickly moved to the side to allow the vehicle to park near us. Dwayne waved his arms high in the air, directing the ambulance as to where to park. Once it came to a stop, the crew quickly exited the vehicle, grabbing their equipment and running down to the beach following Dwayne.

"Thank god you're here," I said, my chest heaving as I stepped away from Sabela so they could assist. Tammy also stood by and let the crew do their job.

"We believe she was stung by a bat ray and has gone into severe anaphylactic shock," she told them as they looked on.

My nerves peaked and sweat poured from my brow with fear. My body shook as I watched a paramedic administer medicine by what I assumed was an EpiPen. They then quickly placed an oxygen mask over her nose and mouth.

He turned and looked at me. "What's the patient's name?"

"She's my wife and her name is Sabela," I said, my voice trembling. "Will she be okay?"

He didn't answer, leaning into Sabela. "Can you hear me, Sabela?" There was no response and her eyes were closed. "Sabela, can you hear me?" the paramedic asked again.

Another paramedic kneeling next to him spoke on his radio, reeling off Sabela's symptoms as two more paramedics walked down to the beach carrying a gurney.

The first paramedic faced me again. "She's in severe anaphylactic shock. We just administered Epinephrine. It should begin to work fairly quickly and reverse the allergic reaction. Her pulse is extremely low. We're going to be taking her to the hospital where she can be closely monitored."

"Can I go with you?" I pleaded.

The paramedic nodded. "Yes, of course."

Tammy reached out and touched my arm. "Don't worry about your things, Dwayne and I will meet you at the hospital and bring them with us. Just go," Tammy said, giving me a little nudge.

I squeezed her hand. "Thank you so much." I watched as the paramedics rolled Sabela onto the gurney and raced her over to the ambulance. Once she was safely inside I jumped in and took a seat across from her. My heart was racing, my breathing strained. "Does this happen often?" I asked the paramedic sitting next to me.

He shook his head. "No, it doesn't. Your wife is an extremely rare case, and so is her allergic reaction. I think the last time someone got stung by a bat ray here was over three years ago. They're pretty docile creatures. Your wife must have spooked it when it was lying in the sand, and as a defense it stung her foot. The stinger is probably still in her foot, but they'll remove it at the hospital."

"But, she's going to be okay?" I asked, desperation emanating from my voice.

"Your wife has had an extremely severe allergic reaction to the poison. Our main concern is that she doesn't go into cardiac arrest. The hospital will give her antihistamine and cortisone to reduce the inflammation of her passageways and help improve her breathing. They'll closely monitor her for the next twenty-four hours."

"Thank you. I don't plan on leaving her side at all tonight."

When we arrived at the small hospital a few minutes later, I stood out of the way so the doctors could do their job and help my wife. I followed closely behind as they wheeled her inside where they were met by a doctor and a nurse. One of the paramedics spoke to the doctor, telling him the treatment they'd given to Sabela, while the nurse walked over to me and gave me a gentle smile.

"Hello, I'm Nurse Blackburn, but you can call me Rachel. Are you a relative of the patient?"

"Yes, I'm her husband. In fact, we're on our honeymoon."

The nurse smiled. "Congratulations. Sabela seems stable and I'm sure she'll be okay. We just need to keep a close eye on her and continue to give her Epinephrine as necessary. We're going to get her settled in a room and make sure she's comfortable. You'll be able to be with her shortly," she informed me. "In the meantime, I'll have you fill out these forms with her information." She handed me a clipboard with papers and pointed to some chairs next to the windows. "You can have a seat over there and I'll come get you after the doctors have attended to her."

"Thank you so much, "I said, feeling somewhat relieved. I walked over to the chairs and took a seat. Concentrating on the paperwork given to me by the nurse, I then heard a female voice call my name.

"Hey Slater, how's Sabela doing?"

I looked up and saw Dwayne and Tammy walking towards me

and smiled. "The doctor thinks she'll be okay. They want her to stay overnight so they can keep an eye on her. They said I'll be able to see her once they've set her up in a room."

Tammy took a seat next to me while Dwayne remained standing. "That's wonderful news," she said with a large smile.

"Thank you so much for coming here, and for helping me on the beach. I had no idea what to do, I was really scared."

Dwayne sat next to Tammy and took her hand. "No problem. I'm glad we were close by."

"Do you guys live here?" I asked.

Dwayne spoke. "Sort of. We live here part-time. We have a small cottage on the island and like to come here during the quieter months when there's not so many tourists. We also have a house in the mountains that my beautiful wife and I built ourselves. It's at a high elevation so we get lots of snow," he chuckled. "Another good reason to come here."

"It's a beautiful island, and our first time here. I just fell in love with the place. In fact, this morning I talked Sabela into going to look at a house that's for sale. The house was amazing, but man, it's way out of our price range, and the real estate lady said that it'll more than likely go for more than the asking price because property is so hard to come by here on the island."

Dwayne nodded and smiled. "Yep, she's right. We bought a small cottage a few years back. It was the only one available, but it's all we need. It's just me, Tammy and our dogs, and we spend most of our time outside or on our boat."

My eyes grew wide. "You have a boat?"

Dwayne chuckled at my reaction. "Yes we do. We have a mooring in the harbor. She's a 60-foot Elliot called Better Endings." He turned and gave Tammy's hand another squeeze. "It's named after one of my wife's books, which helped pay for it," he said with a proud smile.

I looked over at Tammy. "You're an author?"

She smiled and nodded. "Yes I am, and I do most of my writing while I'm here on the island. It's a writer's paradise."

"I'm sure it is," I agreed. I looked at Dwayne. "What do you do?"

"Well, for many years, Tammy and I commercial fished together. When we retired from that, I became a falconer and have been doing it for many years. When we stay on the island, some of my fellow falconer friends board my birds and take care of them."

My jaw dropped. "Wow! You have falcons?"

Dwayne laughed, "I do. Can't be a falconer if you don't have birds," he joked.

"I've never seen a falcon up close."

"Well, we'll have to change that," Dwayne laughed.

"That would be amazing," I said, still shocked by the fact that not only did they have a boat, but falcons, too.

"Tell you what. Once Sabela is back on her feet, we'll have you over for dinner on our boat." He paused. "Do you like to fish? We could even do a fishing trip one day while you're here. We may be retired from the industry, but we still love to fish."

"I think I've only been fishing a couple of times in my entire life," I laughed.

"Something else we need to change," Dwayne stated.

Tammy joined in on the conversation. "How many kids did you say you had? I'm sorry, so much was going on at the beach with Sabela I've forgotten."

"We have twin girls that are six months and Scottie is almost six."

Tammy smiled." Oh, that's right. Now I remember."

"We're actually on our honeymoon, a little delayed because of the girls and their young age."

"Wow! This is turning out to be some honeymoon!" Tammy chuckled.

"It sure is," I replied, rolling my eyes in a joking manner. "It's another reason why I'm so attracted to this place. I would love to raise my kids here; it just feels so safe. But I've discovered that there aren't too many houses big enough for a family of five."

"You're right about that," Tammy agreed. "There were nine offers on our cottage and the final price wasn't cheap."

"You two are really lucky. I envy you."

I'm not sure how long we'd been talking, but we were interrupted by Rachel, the nurse I'd met when we first arrived. She smiled and looked at me. "Slater, you can see Sabela now."

"How's she doing?" I asked.

"She's resting, but conscious and stable."

"Can my friends come with me?" I questioned.

"We can wait here," Tammy suggested.

"No, you won't," I insisted. "I'm not sure if Sabela would even be here if it wasn't for your help and quick reaction. I can't thank you enough, and I'm sure Sabela would like to thank you personally and meet the two people that helped her." I got up out of my chair. "Come on, I want you to meet my amazing wife."

# CHAPTER 18

## SABELA

*I* thought I was dreaming when I heard Slater's voice whisper, "she's sleeping. Maybe we should come back later?"

I strained to speak. My throat was on fire and I felt weak. "I'm awake," I managed to say, straining to open my eyes.

I felt his hand take mine and give it a gentle squeeze. "Hey, how're you doing?"

I gave him a weak smile. "I'm not sure, it hurts to talk." I tried to move but felt constricted. "Where am I?"

Slater squeezed my hand again. "Don't move your other hand. You're in the hospital and you're hooked up to an IV and a blood pressure monitor. Do you remember walking out into the water at the beach?"

I nodded. "Yes, and something bit me."

"It didn't bite you, you got stung by a bat ray and had a severe allergic reaction to the poison from the stinger." Slater moved to the side and looked over at Dwayne and Tammy standing in the room, smiling. "This nice couple came to your rescue and helped me contact 911. I wanted you to meet them."

I looked beyond Slater and smiled at them. "Thank you for helping Slater and I, I only wished we'd met under better circumstances."

They approached the other side of the bed, holding hands and smiling down at me.

Dwayne said, "hi there. I'm Dwayne, and this is my wife Tammy. We're just glad to see you're doing okay. You had us all worried there for a while." He paused and projected another friendly smile. "I told Slater when you're feeling better, we'll get together for dinner."

I managed another weak smile. "That would be lovely. Thank you."

Slater gently brushed my hair back away from my face. "I was so scared, Sabela. Dwayne kept me calm, and he and Tammy both stayed with me in the waiting room until we were able to see you. I would have gone crazy sitting out there by myself worrying about you."

"When can I leave? Are we still on Catalina?" I asked, my brow furrowed.

Slater gave me a softhearted smile and squeezed my hand. "Yes, we're still on our honeymoon on the island. They want to keep you here overnight because you had such a severe allergic reaction to the poison. They said I can stay with you. They'll bring a cot so I can sleep here in the room with you, but not until after they've given you a second dose of medication in a few hours. They're also monitoring your blood pressure because it dropped so drastically."

I was stunned. "Wow, I've never been allergic to anything. This is a first; I can't get over how weak I feel."

Dwayne spoke up and said, "it's normal for you to feel weak and tired. Your body's been through a lot. It may take a few days for you to regain your strength, even after you've left the hospital. The rest of your honeymoon may be spent resting, I'm afraid."

"Really? I'm going to be feeling like this for the next few days?"

I looked at Slater with sadness in my eyes. "I'm so sorry I ruined our honeymoon."

Slater looked shocked by my words as he leaned in and gave me a gentle kiss on the lips. His warm lips soothed me. "Sweetheart, you didn't ruin anything. I'm relieved that you're going to be okay. I was so scared. You couldn't breathe, and I had no idea what to do. Right now, I am the happiest man alive because I'm here holding your hand and talking to you, and I get to tell you how much I love you. For a while I was afraid I wouldn't be able to. I was truly scared."

"I love you, too." I turned and looked at Dwayne and Tammy. "Thank you again."

"No need to thank us," Dwayne replied with a friendly smile. "Like your husband said, we're just glad you'll be okay. Now we're going to leave you two honeymooners alone. Slater, I've already put my number in your phone after I called the ambulance, so give us a call later and we'll bring you something to eat while you're here with Sabela."

"You did? I was just about to ask you for your number. Thanks, I'll definitely call you," Slater replied.

After they'd left, I closed my eyes and tried to move my achy foot. "My foot really hurts," I moaned.

"That's where you got stung when you were wading in the water. The doctor said they'd removed the stinger, but it may take a few days for the swelling to go down and that it'd be extremely sore."

I closed my eyes, trying to deflect the pain. "Well, he's right about that, it hurts to move it."

"Just lay still and rest. Close your eyes and get some sleep. I'm not going anywhere," Slater said in a soothing voice, taking a seat next to my bed.

My eyes felt heavy as he spoke to me. I strained to keep them open, but soon felt myself drifting off to sleep like Slater had suggested.

The next thing I remember was hearing voices all around me. One I knew was Slater's, but the female voice I didn't recognize.

I opened my eyes and saw Slater talking to a nurse. He looked over at me when the nurse whispered, "she's awake, her eyes are open," as she walked over to the machines next to the bed. "Sabela, can you hear me? I'm Nurse Rachel."

I turned my head and looked at her before nodding. "Yes, I can hear you. How long have I been sleeping?"

"About three hours," Slater replied. "You looked so peaceful and beautiful. I didn't take my eyes off of you the whole time," he said with a loving smile.

"Wow, I must have been tired."

"I'm going to give you another round of meds, we don't want you having a relapse," Nurse Rachel proclaimed as she prepped the needle.

"Are you in any pain?" Slater asked, trying to distract me from what the nurse was doing.

"My throat is still sore and so is my foot."

"That's normal," Rachel replied, administering the medicine into my thigh.

I tried to remain relaxed when I felt the pinch of the needle. I squeezed Slater's hand for support, and he squeezed mine back and rubbed my forehead. "She's all done," he whispered a few seconds later.

After Nurse Rachel had left, Slater propped up my pillows and helped me sit up. "They're going to bring you some food soon. Are you hungry?" he asked.

I nodded. "I am. I don't think I've eaten all day. What about you?"

"Dwayne and Tammy are on their way back here and are picking me up a cheeseburger."

"They seem really nice. Do they live here?"

"Part time. They like to come here when the island isn't so crowded with tourists. They have a small cottage in town, and they have a boat anchored out in the harbor where they spend most of their time."

"Wow, that's cool!"

"Yes, and they've invited us on their boat for dinner when you're feeling better. It's called Better Endings after one of Tammy's books."

I shifted my body, trying to find a comfortable spot and ease the pain I felt in my foot. "She's an author?"

"Yes, and Dwayne's a falconer. They've commercial fished for lobsters together for many years and have been coming to the island every year for the past twenty-five years."

"They must love it here," I replied.

Slater nodded. "Dwayne said there's no better place. I still think this would be a wonderful place to raise our family."

I released a heavy sigh. "Oh Slater, are you still obsessed with that idea? I don't see how we can afford it."

Slater squeezed my hand. "I know. I'm sorry, I'll drop it. I'm just dreaming again," he joked.

Nurse Rachel returned with a tray of food consisting of baked chicken, green beans, mashed potatoes and strawberry Jell-O for dessert. After setting the tray in front of me, she told us a porter would be in shortly with a cot for Slater. We thanked her, then Slater set up my tray and poured water from the pitcher for me. A few minutes later there was a knock at the door.

"Come in," Slater called out, looking at the door.

Dwayne and Tammy entered the room, both wearing blue jeans and white t-shirts.

"Hey, how's the patient doing?" Tammy asked, handing Slater a bag of food.

Slater took the bag and placed the contents on my tray next to my food. "She's doing great!" Slater replied with a big smile, picking up the cheeseburger. "Pull up a chair and you can watch us eat," he said with a laugh.

Dwayne pulled up two chairs from under the window and

placed them at the end of my bed. Tammy took a seat and handed Dwayne a bottle of water she'd been carrying. After sitting down next to Tammy, he took a sip, smiled at Slater and said, "here's to new friends."

Slater raised his bottle of water and nodded. "To new friends."

I picked up my plastic cup and smiled at the nice couple that had come into our lives, feeling ever so grateful. "To new friends - I hope we stay in touch after our honeymoon is over."

Dwayne smiled and winked. "Oh, you can count on it."

# CHAPTER 19

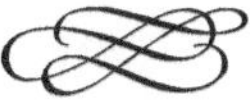

## SLATER

*D*wayne and Tammy stayed for another hour after we'd eaten, regaling us with their fishing tales and stories about building their house in the mountains from the ground up. Sabela and I were fascinated with their adventures and laughed out loud at many of them. We were also anxious to read a book they'd written together called Waves and Memories. I'm not much of a reader, but when Tammy told me it was a collection of short stories about their fishing days, I knew it was right up my alley.

"Wow! You guys have led quite the life," I said, wiping away tears of laughter after hearing some of the hilarious stories.

"It's been quite an adventure," Dwayne said, wrapping his arms around Tammy's waist and smiling into her eyes. "And there's many more stories that I haven't told you about in the book." He leaned back in his chair, stretching his legs out in front of him and resting his hands behind his head. "Our dream has always been to buy a boat and name it after one of Tammy's books. We recently bought a 68-foot Elliot, got rid of our smaller boats and now just have the one. She's amazing," Dwayne said with a proud grin, "and the name is perfect, Better Endings. We've always dreamt big, but I think this was one of our biggest dreams." He gave us a big grin. "But we've achieved it. It never hurts to dream big - it gives you goals and the inspiration to work hard."

"That's awesome," Sabela said excitedly. "Your boat sounds amazing, and we'll have to get a copy of your book. I'd love to read it."

Tammy smiled at Sabela. "We'll make sure you get a copy." She rubbed Dwayne's thigh, "we should get going. Sabela needs her rest."

Dwayne nodded and stood up. "You're right. If you feel up to it Sabela, we'd still love to have you both on the boat for dinner tomorrow night. We could pick you up in our skiff at the dinghy dock."

"That'd be great!" Sabela replied, smiling. "I should be feeling much better by then I hope."

Dwayne shook my hand. "How does 7:00 pm sound?" he asked. "You can call me when you're heading over to the dock, I'll come over and pick you up."

"Sounds great," I said, giving Tammy a friendly hug before they left.

"They're so nice," Sabela said, taking a sip of water.

"Yeah, they sure are. I'm looking forward to seeing their boat tomorrow."

A few minutes later there was a knock at the door and a hospital porter entered the room wheeling in a cot and bedding. I took the bedding from him and watched as he set up the cot and proceeded to make the bed. "Thank you," I said, as he took Sabela's tray and informed us there was a nurse at the desk around the clock if we needed anything. I thanked him and adjusted Sabela's pillows as she slid her body beneath the covers until she was lying flat. "Get some sleep, okay?" I whispered in her ear, giving her a light kiss on the lips.

She nodded, gave me a tender smile, and closed her eyes.

I stood and stared at her for a few minutes, admiring her

beauty. Then I crawled under the covers of the cot fully clothed, and fell asleep dreaming of the big house for sale on the island.

Sabela slept through the night, unlike me, who found the cot extremely uncomfortable as I tossed and turned all night.

When I woke the next morning, I was surprised to see Sabela wide awake and sitting up in bed. I rubbed my eyes and yawned before attempting to move my aching, cramped body. "Hey, what time is it?" I asked, smiling as I pulled myself up and out of the uncomfortable cot. It felt good to walk and stretch my legs after having them bent at the knees all night.

She picked up her phone and glanced at the screen, "five-thirty," she replied.

I walked over and sat on the edge of the bed and rubbed her arm. "Have you been awake long? How are you feeling?"

"I don't know how long I've been awake. Maybe half an hour. I didn't want to wake you, and I've just been sitting here scanning my phone calls. We need to call my mom. She's left three messages, and the last message she left she sounded pretty worried. She said the kids are fine, but she's concerned because we've not answered any of her calls."

"Oh shit! With everything that's happened to you, I never thought about calling her. It's my fault. I should have called and let her know what's going on. You've been out of it."

Sabela smiled. "It's okay, I'll call her in a bit. I wonder what time they'll bring breakfast? I'm starving."

I chuckled. "Well, you're definitely feeling better. You've got an appetite, that's for sure."

"I am. My throat is still feeling a little scratchy, but not like yesterday, and the swelling's gone down in my foot. It's not hurting as much."

Her words relieved me. "That's great! We're still going to take it easy today, though. No swimming, kayaking or snorkeling for a day or two."

"To be honest, I have no desire to go in the ocean for a while. I don't care if we spend the rest of our honeymoon lying on the beach," she confessed.

I patted her arm. "That's fine with me too, and I completely understand. Whatever you want to do. You know me, I'll go along with anything you'd like."

Sabela called her mom a few hours later after we'd both eaten the breakfasts provided by the hospital. I was surprised how good the sausage omelet was, and how sweet and fresh the side of fruit tasted.

Sabela's mom, Charlotte, was horrified at first when we told her that Sabela was calling from the hospital, but when we told her what'd happened, we were both surprised to learn that her father'd been stung by a bat ray many years before Sabela was born, and had the same severe reaction which had landed him in the hospital. It was something Sabela never knew about her father, as well as the fact that he always carried an EpiPen in the glove compartment of his truck. Sabela now understood where her allergies came from.

"Yes, Sabela, the hospital will probably give you an EpiPen before you leave the hospital, and you will need to carry it with you always. It will save your life if you ever go into anaphylactic shock again. Thank god for that nice couple who were close by," her mom told her.

"Yes Mom, they've invited us for dinner tonight on their boat. It should be a lot of fun," Sabela said, then perked up her ears. "Oh no, I hear one of the girls crying in the background. I sure do miss them. Are you sure you're managing okay?" Sabela asked, sounding concerned. "It sounds like you're feeling better," she added.

"I am, and besides, being around the girls and Scottie everyday does wonders for Lorenzo and I. We're fine, now don't you worry. You just get well. I'm going to go feed the girls. Call me tomorrow. I love you."

"I love you too, Mom," Sabela said, ending the call.

After checking on Sabela numerous times and seeing that her

blood pressure had returned to normal, they released her at noon much to our relief. As Charlotte predicted, they gave her two EpiPens and spent a few moments giving her instructions on how to use it.

"I have to give myself an injection?" Sabela gasped.

"Yes, if no one is with you, and you must do it quickly. No time to think about it," Nurse Rachel told her.

Sabela looked my way, horrified. "That's it, you're coming with me wherever I go," she joked.

After saying goodbye to the small staff that we'd gotten to know quite well, and on a first name basis, one of the nurses wheeled Sabela out in a wheelchair, where a golf cart was waiting to take us back to the hotel.

Behind the front desk of the hotel, Karen greeted us with a friendly smile. "Where have you two been? The housekeeper said your room has not been touched since yesterday morning. I was going to put out a search team for you," she laughed. She then proceeded to answer the phone before we could answer.

"Good morning. Thank you for calling the Avalon Hotel, this is Karen Wright speaking, how may I help you?"

After Karen had ended the call, we told her the events of the past day and that I'd stayed at the hospital with Sabela.

She held her chest in disbelief. "Well, I'm here all day, so if there's anything you need just let me know. We can even bring lunch to you if you'd like. There's a menu in the drawer of the end table in your room."

"That'd be great, thank you. We plan to spend the entire day in our room so Sabela can rest. This evening we've been invited for dinner on Dwayne and Tammy's boat." I paused, "it's called Better Endings. Do you know them?"

Karen released a big grin and said, "I do know them. They're a wonderful couple. They live here part time. Been coming here for years."

"They're great. Dwayne helped me when Sabela went into shock on the beach. He was amazing."

"Well, you were lucky they were there. If that had happened to me, that's the couple I'd want to save me. They commercial fished together for many years and are very informative when it comes to the ocean and what lurks beneath," she laughed. "Now, go on up to your room and call me if you need anything."

I smiled. "Thank you so much, and we will." I said, taking Sabela's hand.

# CHAPTER 20

## SABELA

When we entered the room, Slater immediately walked over to the French doors and opened them. The fresh salty air quickly entered the room, and I breathed in the refreshing scent, filling my lungs.

"Do you want to lie on the bed or sit outside on the balcony?" Slater asked as he put my bags on the leather couch.

"I think I want to sit outside. I've been cooped up in that hospital bed for so long it would feel great to sit outside and do some people-watching."

"Sounds good to me. I'll meet you out there in a few minutes. I'm going to call Dwayne and let him know we're back at the hotel, and that we'll meet them for dinner tonight." He paused. "You feel up to it, right?"

I nodded. "Yes, I want to see their boat," I laughed. "I'm not missing that."

It felt good to be out of the hospital and in the privacy of our hotel room. I still felt weak and wasn't up to any outdoor activities, and my throat was still a bit sore, but talking had become easier, and my foot was no longer in pain.

It was yet another glorious day on the island. The skies were a brilliant blue with no clouds, and there was a slight breeze, which I gladly welcomed. I took a seat on the balcony and looked out at the ocean. I spotted a few fishing boats and lots of kayaks out around the harbor. The atmosphere was peaceful and calming. I understood Slater's infatuation with this place. I'm not going to deny that I wouldn't mind waking up to this every day and spending our weekends on the beach with the kids. But for me it was an impossible dream, and I've never have been much of a dreamer. I didn't allow it to consume me like it has Slater.

I spent the next half hour taking in the view of the boats in the harbor, watching the masts of the sailboats sway in the breeze. The beach was quiet, with a few people soaking up rays. I cringed when I saw a couple walk into the water, expecting to hear piercing screams from being stung by a bat ray. It was obvious that I'd been traumatized by the event and was not about to rush back into the water any time soon.

Slater joined me, smiling, and took a seat next to me. "It's all set. Dwayne will pick us up at the dinghy dock at 6:00 pm tonight. In the meantime, the entire day is ours to relax and take it easy."

***

It was a short, pleasant walk from the hotel to the dinghy dock. The evening was still warm, and I chose to dress casually in jeans, white sandals and a white cotton top. At the last minute I grabbed a light blue sweater in case it got cooler, draping it over my shoulders. Slater led the way, dressed in beige shorts and a white t-shirt, holding my hand. I spotted Dwayne standing in his white dinghy as we approached the ramp. He waved and smiled, and we both waved back.

"I hope you haven't been waiting too long," Slater said, stepping onto the dock.

Dwayne shook his head. "No, I just got here." He looked over at me and smiled. "How are you feeling, Sabela?"

I returned the friendly smile. "Much better, thank you."

He held out his hand as I stepped onto the dinghy. I giggled when it began to rock from my weight. Dwayne continued to hold my hand as I steadied my feet and gained my balance before taking a seat. Slater followed, sitting next to me and taking my hand.

"Well, Tammy is fixing a feast of fresh seafood and salad, my favorite," he laughed. "Our boat is at the far end of the harbor. We'll be there in a few minutes," he said, firing up the dinghy and untying the line.

I spotted their boat from a distance as Dwayne weaved through the harbor amongst the many boats tied up to their moorings. I knew it was their boat when I saw the name Better Endings painted in big, bold blue letters on the stern. "I see your boat," I said to Dwayne. "She's beautiful, and I love the name, it's perfect."

Dwayne smiled with pride. "Yeah, she's a beauty. Other than our son Matt, she's our pride and joy," Dwayne joked.

"She's huge," Slater remarked as Dwayne slowed down and pulled up to the stern of Better Endings, tying off the dinghy to a cleat before shutting down the motor.

"She's a 68-foot Elliot which is probably the max Tammy and I can handle on our own. Any bigger and we'd have to get a crew, and Tammy and I didn't want to do that. We enjoy the solitude of just her and I on the boat; fishing, snorkeling and just cruising up and down the island."

"Sounds like the perfect lifestyle," Slater said, helping me onto the swim step.

"We have no complaints," Dwayne chuckled, following us onto the boat.

We were greeted by Tammy standing on the deck of the boat wearing a large friendly smile, dressed in Levi capris and a loose, sky-blue blouse. "Hello and welcome aboard," she said, as we stepped onto the large teak deck, complete with a huge oval-shaped bait tank in the center. At her feet were two excited dogs, a Brittany and a Jack Russell who started barking excitedly as I stepped onto the deck.

I returned the smile and met her in a friendly hug. "Thank you, this is amazing!" I said, scanning the deck and looking at the teak steps that led to an upper deck and a flywheel.

Tammy followed my eyes. "That's where we store the dinghy when traveling, and it also makes for a great sun deck when the dinghy's in the water," she told me as she picked up the Jack Russell who continued to bark. "This is Miss Ellie, who even though is in her senior years, is still the best watchdog, and the Brittany is Miss Tess."

I looked up at the upper deck. "The view must be amazing from up there, no matter where you're docked," I said, letting Miss Ellie sniff my hand. "You are so cute," I said to the friendly dog, petting her head.

"Come on inside and I'll show you the rest of the boat," Tammy said, smiling.

Slater remained outside with Dwayne, showing him fishing poles and the inside of the bait tank which I found amusing; I never knew that Slater liked to fish since I'd known him.

Tammy set Miss Ellie on the deck, and both dogs followed us into the galley. I was surprised how spacious it was. The color scheme was a light beige and white. To my right was a large, oval beige couch and table, and on my left was a counter spanning the entire length of the galley with lots of cupboards for storage underneath. The galley kitchen was much bigger than I'd imagined, separated by a bar. I was also surprised to see that it had all the comforts of home, including a full-size stainless-steel fridge, microwave, stove countertop and two ovens.

"This is incredible," I gasped. "Why have a cottage on the island when you have this?" I asked, amazed by all the luxuries.

"Oh, several reasons. Sometimes we're here for weeks at a time, and we have these two spoiled dogs that need a small yard. It's also nice to break away from the boat occasionally and live like regular folk," she joked.

We were soon joined by Dwayne and Slater. Tammy pulled out some fixings from the fridge and a pitcher of iced tea. Dwayne took us down to the sleeping quarters and showed us the spacious master stateroom with a queen size bed and its own head, as well as three other staterooms with single bunkbeds.

"Wow, this sleeps a lot of people," Slater said, leading the way back up to the galley.

"Yes, it will sleep eight comfortably," Dwayne remarked, approaching Tammy from behind and wrapping his arms around her waist, giving her a kiss on the neck.

"Something smells really good. What's for dinner?" Tammy giggled from his touch and leaned into his embrace. "We're having steamed seafood, rice and fresh vegetables. There's glasses and a pitcher of iced tea on the table," she said, stirring the rice.

"Can I help you with anything?" I offered. Tammy shook her head. "No, I have everything under control. We'll be eating in about fifteen minutes. Go grab some iced tea and make yourself comfortable," Tammy instructed me, stirring the rice again.

I joined Slater and Dwayne at the table. Dwayne poured me a tall glass of chilled iced tea. "Thanks," I said, taking a seat.

"So, how often do you come over here?" Slater asked, taking a sip of his drink.

"As often as we can," Dwayne chuckled. "Like I said before, we tend to come when it's not peak season and full of tourists. Tammy gets a lot of her writing done here, and I'll take the dinghy out and get some fishing in. Our son Matt visits on weekends while we're here with his wife and two boys."

"Do you think you'll ever live here full-time?" Slater asked.

"We've talked about it and would sure love to, maybe one day. But I have the five falcons and do bird abatement, and you can't fly birds here on the island. They'd probably end up back on the mainland," he joked.

Slater leaned back in his chair and looked around the comfortable boat. "Well, I'm sure envious. You guys have it made."

Dwayne gave Slater a hard stare. "You sure have fallen hard for this place, haven't you?"

I intervened in the conversation while rolling my eyes. "That's an understatement. It's all he's talked about since we got off the ferry. He's obsessed with this island, even though I've told him repeatedly that we could never afford anything here."

Dwayne turned to me and gave me the same stare. "Do you like it here? Could you see yourself living here with Slater and your kids?"

I shrugged my shoulders. "Well, yes, it's beautiful, but why dwell on something you can never have?" I replied.

Dwayne nodded. "You have a point, but I always say, never say never. Tammy and I have dreamt about this boat for many years. If we thought we could never have obtained it, then we wouldn't be sitting here right now, and more than likely we'd never have met you two." He leaned back against the seat and spread his arms across the back. "You gotta dream big."

I was suddenly embarrassed by Dwayne's remark. Probably because he made a lot of sense. I had immediately tossed out Slater's crazy idea and refused to give it any thought; I shrugged my shoulders again. "Well, what I mean is, we can't afford to live here right now."

Slater turned and looked at me, his eyes wide. "So, if we could afford to live here, you'd consider it?"

"Well, yeah, I guess, but we can't, so why keep talking about it?"

"Because it's good to have dreams," Dwayne replied. "It's what gives us motivation, and the will to strive for the things we want. Don't you agree?"

I nodded. "Yes, I do agree." I smiled at Slater. "I'm sorry I brushed off your idea so quickly. I won't quit dreaming, okay? Maybe one day we'll talk about living here."

Slater grinned and patted my thigh. "Awesome. Let's keep the dream alive, okay?"

"Okay."

Tammy called from the galley. "Okay guys, the food's ready. Come and get it."

For the next hour we sat around the table, feasting on a delicious dinner as Dwayne and Tammy shared more fishing stories, and I told them about our group of friends that were like family to us back home.

"I'd love to meet them," Tammy said, as we both cleared the dishes and took them to the galley.

"I would love that too," I said, smiling. "When do you go back to the mainland?"

"Next week. We could get together over the following weekend if you'd like?"

"That would be great. I can cook us all dinner," I said excitedly and then a thought occurred to me. "Shoot, our condo is too small to have everyone over for dinner. I'll talk to Claire and see if we can have it at her place, which is technically ours, but they run the children's home, Open Arms, which I told you about over dinner."

"I think it's an amazing thing what you've done, and yes, if Claire's okay with it, that'd be great," Tammy said, grinning.

I clapped my hands. "Oh, I'm so excited. I know you're just going to love everyone, and I know they'll all love the two of you."

"We're looking forward to it," Tammy said as she stood up. "What do you say we continue this conversation outside on the deck where we can enjoy the cool night and the beautiful stars?"

Dwayne stood, picking up his glass. "You always have the best ideas. I'm right behind you, honey."

Slater and I followed them out onto the deck and immediately released a sigh. The skies had turned dark, lit only by the twinkles of the stars and a sliver of moon. There was a slight breeze that blew through my hair, tickling my neck and cheeks.

"Are you warm enough?" Dwayne asked as I glanced around at the beautiful harbor.

I nodded and smiled. "I am, thank you. The air is still warm, even though it's dark out."

"Yes, it doesn't get too cold here. We spend most evenings out here on the deck, just taking it all in," Tammy replied, as she took a seat on one of the teak deck chairs Dwayne had set out while we were talking. "It's one of the best places to write a book," she added.

"I bet. What a great environment to get your creative juices flowing," I replied.

"It beats an office with walls," Tammy laughed.

I looked out at the surrounding boats, some lit up with people sitting on their decks like us, enjoying the tranquility of the island and the gentle rocking of the waters beneath us. The small town of Avalon was lit up with lights from the houses and restaurants that were still open. Soft music played, and many people were still walking along the street.

I leaned back in my chair, took Slater's hand, and closed my eyes. I can't remember the last time I felt this relaxed. Slater squeezed my hand and then suddenly let go when he heard a phone ring.

"Is that your phone?" he asked Dwayne and Tammy. Both shook their heads. "Nope, not our ring tones," Dwayne said. "Sounds like it's coming from inside the galley."

I quickly sat up and pinned my ears. "That's my phone. My purse is down below. I'll be right back," I replied, as I stood up and went in search of my purse.

Inside the galley, I followed the sound of the ringtone and found my purse on the bench of the table. Pulling out my phone, I was surprised to see Claire's name on the screen. My first thought was concerns about her pregnancy, and I quickly answered the call. "Hey Claire, what's up? Everything okay?"

"Hi Sabela, I hope I'm not calling too late. I really wish I didn't have to because you're on your honeymoon."

My body became tense. "What's going on, Claire?"

There was a moment of silence before she spoke, and I sensed her hesitation.

"I think you need to come home. Your mother's not well."

# CHAPTER 21

## SABELA

ear swept through me as I held my chest and allowed Claire to continue.

"Jill is at your house helping Lorenzo with the kids. We, meaning me, Jill and Sadie, promised we would take turns going over there to help them out. Sadie was there yesterday. I just got off the phone with Jill and she sounded worried, so I decided to call you," Claire said, her voice tense.

"What? Oh my god! She wasn't feeling well when we left, but she insisted she was okay, and when I spoke with her earlier she said she was fine."

Claire took a deep breath. "I don't think she's being completely honest with you, or Lorenzo for that matter. He'd asked Jill not to say anything to you because he didn't want to ruin your honeymoon or worry you, so Jill called me, but I didn't agree with Lorenzo and decided to call you. I hope you're not upset with me."

"What? No, of course I'm not upset. I'm glad you did."

"I hope it's nothing serious, but I felt you should know. Are you going to call them?" Claire asked.

"No, because If I do, they'll just pretend everything is okay and insist we not come home. I'm going to tell Slater that we need to leave ASAP. I just don't know how. It's nighttime, and the next ferry doesn't leave here until early morning." I let out a heavy sigh. "I need to figure this out. I'll keep you posted - thank you for letting me know."

After ending the call, I shoved my phone back into my purse and raced up to the deck. My palms were sweaty and I clasped them together as I joined the others, interrupting Dwayne and Tammy's conversation. I stood next to Slater's chair and looked at him with sadness in my eyes. "I'm sorry, but we need to go home, there's something wrong with my mom."

Slater stood up and immediately took me into his arms to comfort me as I tried to hold back my tears. "What's wrong with her? Do you know?" he asked.

I shook my head. "I have no idea, but for Claire to call me because she's worried has me concerned. Jill is at our house right now, and she called Claire because she's worried, too. Please Slater, I want to go home, but I don't know how. The ferry doesn't leave until morning."

Dwayne spoke next. "We can take you. I can have this boat ready in an hour."

I was shocked. "Really? You'd do that for us? We need to go back to the hotel and pack first."

"That's fine, I'll take you back to the dock in the dinghy and pick you up in an hour. In the meantime, Tammy and I will get the boat ready for the crossing. After we pick you up, we will just need to hoist the dinghy onto the boat."

I was speechless. "Thank you so much, I'm not sure what to say. It's been one thing after another on this honeymoon, and each time you've saved the day."

"It's my pleasure. I'm happy to help. We'll anchor at the guest dock in the marina. From there you should be able to call an Uber.

We can spend the night on the boat and head back here in the morning."

Dwayne wasted no time, and within fifteen minutes he'd dropped us off at the dinghy dock, and we rushed back to the hotel. Karen, the friendly receptionist we had gotten to know since arriving, had already gone home for the night, so we explained to the young, blonde gentlemen behind the desk why we had to check out early. He expressed his concerns, and, to our surprise, gave us credit for seven days to use anytime within the year.

"Thank you so much!" Slater replied. "We'll definitely be back, we love it here!"

After gathering our things from our room and making sure we hadn't left anything behind, we were back at the dinghy dock ten minutes early, waiting for Dwayne to return.

Slater held me tight as we stood on the dock and waited. He kissed the top of my head, his arm over my shoulder, my head on his chest. "How're you doing?" he said as he rubbed my shoulder and kissed my cheek. "We'll be home before midnight."

"I'm okay. I'm just worried about my mom, but I'm also angry with her for not being honest with me. Why couldn't she just tell me she wasn't feeling well? We could have postponed this trip until she was feeling better."

"Maybe she thought she'd be feeling better soon, and I'm sure she didn't want to ruin our trip."

"Well, her not being honest with me has ruined the trip." I shook my head. "I'm sorry. I'm sure she has her reasons. I'm lashing out because I'm worried about her."

A few minutes later Dwayne pulled up to the dock, and after boarding Better Endings, Tammy and Dwayne hoisted the dinghy onto the upper deck and covered it. We then headed out of the harbor.

After holding me for a while and doing his best to comfort me as we stood outside on the deck, Slater joined Dwayne in the wheelhouse, where Dwayne let Slater drive the boat for a while before switching to autopilot.

I joined Tammy in the galley where she did her best to preoccupy me with small talk, but I couldn't focus, and my smiles were forced. My mind was consumed with worry over my mom, and until I could be by her side and have answers, I knew I wouldn't be able to relax.

# CHAPTER 22

## SLATER

Sabela was consumed with worry, and it tore at my heart to see her so stressed, not knowing the condition of her mom. Like her, I also felt helpless and couldn't wait to get back home.

After she'd settled in the galley with Tammy, she insisted I go up to the wheelhouse, not only to check it out but to keep Dwayne company, too. I hesitated at first, but Sabela was adamant, and knew I had been dying to see the wheelhouse in action.

"I'm fine, honest. There's no sense in us all moping here in the galley. This is your first time on a luxury boat like this. I don't want to deprive you of enjoying it. There's nothing we can do until we're home. Please, go keep Dwayne company," Sabela insisted.

I gave her a caring smile, wrapped my arms around her waist and kissed her gently on the lips. "Okay. You know where I'll be if you need anything. I love you."

She gave me a weak smile and kissed me back. "I love you, too."

Once up in the wheelhouse, Dwayne looked over his shoulder and smiled, both hands resting on the wheel at the helm. "How's Sabela doing?"

I joined him and looked out at the dark ocean surrounding us. "She's doing okay. Man, it sure is dark out here."

"Yep, no streetlights to guide the way. But all this technology will," he chuckled, pointing at the dash. He took one hand off the wheel. "Do you want to take over?"

My jaw dropped and I patted my chest. "Me? I've never driven a boat before."

"Oh, there's nothing to it. I'll let you take the wheel for a minute or two before I switch it to autopilot just so you can see what it feels like, and you can tell people you drove a 67-foot Elliot."

I stood next to him at the helm and Dwayne stepped aside, allowing me to take the wheel. He then began pointing to many of the electronics on the dash, explaining each one's function. I was fascinated, and understood why Dwayne and Tammy enjoyed this lifestyle. A sense of freedom came with it. An open ocean without the headaches of society breathing down your neck at every corner. Here there was just peace, your choices and your time. Why hadn't I discovered this life sooner?

An hour later we were pulling up to a guest dock in San Diego Harbor. I watched as Tammy jumped off the boat onto the dock and quickly secured the lines to the cleats. "You guys make a great team," I hollered from the wheelhouse.

Tammy looked up from the dock. "Been doing this for years. We both know our places on the boat," she laughed.

I turned to Dwayne and held out my hand. "Thank you so much, for everything."

Dwayne took my hand and shook it. "Hey, it's our pleasure. I sure hope Sabela's mom is okay. I'll call you an Uber, and Tammy and I will spend the night at the dock here and head back to Catalina tomorrow morning. Call us and let us know how her mom is doing, and hopefully we can still meet next week for dinner."

"I sure will. I'll call you as soon as I know anything, and yes, we'd still like to get together next week," I said, following him through the door of the wheelhouse and down onto the deck where Sabela was talking to Tammy.

"Hey hon, Dwayne's called us an Uber. They're picking us up outside the Bayfront Restaurant in fifteen minutes."

"Great!" Sabela replied. "Our bags are inside the galley."

"Do you need help getting them?" Tammy asked.

I shook my head. "No, I got it." I turned to Tammy and smiled. "Thank you again for helping us," I laughed, rolling my eyes. "I'm not sure what we'd have done without you."

I wrapped my arms around Sabela's waist to keep out the chilled air and carried one of the bags with my free hand while Sabela carried the other two. When we reached the top of the ramp, we turned and waved at Dwayne and Tammy standing on the deck of their boat, who smiled and waved back.

"I'm so happy we met those guys," Sabela said, as we walked through the parking lot looking for the Bayfront Restaurant.

"Me too. I'd like to keep in touch with them. They're still hoping to come for dinner next week."

"I'm sure we can make it happen. I'll be much better once I know what's going on with my mom."

I gave her a caring smile. "I know, sweetheart. I see the restaurant up ahead. Let's go stand in front of it."

"Hey, I just had a thought. Our car is still at the Ferry Terminal. When are we going to get it?" Saber asked.

"I thought about that, and I'll have Ricky give me a ride in the next day or so."

I was pleased that the Uber was right on time, and within the hour we were pulling up outside our condo. I glanced at my watch. "Wow, it's after midnight. We'll have to be quiet going inside. I don't want to startle anyone, and we'll have to sleep on the hide-a-way bed downstairs."

Sabela stepped out of the car and stared at our home. "The

lights are on downstairs. Someone is up," she said, waiting for the Uber driver to get our bags out of the trunk.

After thanking the driver and watching him drive away, we headed up to the front door. Using my key, I quietly unlocked it and opened the door. I immediately saw Lorenzo sitting in the recliner holding one of the twins. He looked up, shocked to see us entering the condo. "What are you two doing here?" he asked, his brow creased.

Sabela set down the bags she was carrying by the front door and walked over to where Lorenzo sat. She reached out and gently stroked who she now saw was Hope's hair. "I heard Mom is not feeling well and got worried. Why didn't you tell me? And what's wrong with Hope?"

"Hope was fussing, so I brought her down here so she wouldn't wake Joy or Charlotte, and I've been rocking her." He smiled. "She's sound asleep now." He gave Sabela a hard stare. "Why did you not call first? There was no need to cut your honeymoon short. We are fine."

"That's not what I heard. Jill called Claire out of concern, and Claire called me. Apparently, you told Jill not to say anything to us. What's going on, Lorenzo? What's wrong with my mom?"

I quietly set down the bag next to the ones Sabela had left by the door, joining them in the living room. Lorenzo continued to rock Hope while he spoke, but his tone was weak and unconvincing, like he was hiding something. "I said that to Jill because I was afraid of this. That you would come home worried and ruin your honeymoon, and you did. I was right."

Sabela's tone was sharp, but she kept it at a loud whisper so as not to wake Hope. "Of course, I'm worried, Lorenzo. I was miles away across the ocean on an island with no answers. You never called me. I had no idea what's going on or how sick Mom is, so yes, I needed to come home." Sabela scanned the room. "Is she upstairs sleeping?"

Lorenzo nodded. "Yes."

"So, what's going on? Does she have a cold, the flu, a bug?" Sabela asked, unable to hide the frustration in her voice.

I noticed Lorenzo avoiding eye contact with Sabela. "I think you should be having this conversation with Charlotte."

Fear swept over Sabela's face, and I took her hand. "So it's serious? It's more than a cold?"

Chills ran through my body. Lorenzo's body language was telling me it could be serious, and I felt Sabela's body tremble against mine. I pulled her in and wrapped my arm around her waist, waiting for Lorenzo to reply.

"Please Sabela, let your mother tell you. I promised that I would let her."

Sabela's body continued to tremble, and I moved my arm up to her shoulder and stroked it as she spoke. "Lorenzo, you're scaring me. What's going on?"

I didn't like the fact that we were putting Lorenzo on the spot; even though we both needed to know, I felt that it wasn't his place to tell us. He was right, it was Charlotte's place, and she'd already asked Lorenzo not to say anything. She, too wanted to be the one to tell us. I turned and looked at Sabela.

"Sweetheart, we aren't being fair to Lorenzo. Let's not do this to him. He's right; whatever is going on with your mother, she's obviously made it clear to Lorenzo that she wants to be the one to tell us. We should respect that and wait until morning."

Sabela pulled away and rubbed her eyes. "How am I supposed to sleep, not knowing what's wrong with my mom?"

I raised my hand to quiet her. "Shhh, you're going to wake up Hope. I'm sorry Sabela, but it's the right thing to do. We must think of your mom's wishes and not what we want. We need to put her first. Normally I would go along with everything you want, but not this time, and I'm sorry. Please understand, I don't want to upset Charlotte and force Lorenzo to go against her wishes, and, like I said, this is truly unfair to him."

Lorenzo whispered. "Thank you, Slater. You are correct. Charlotte did ask me not to say anything and I am always true to my word."

"Thank you Lorenzo, I respect that," I told him, taking Sabela's hand again.

Sabela wiped a tear from her eye and squeezed my hand. "I'm sorry, I know you're right. It's just really hard, but I agree." She looked at Lorenzo. "I'm sorry. I didn't mean to pressure you. Do you want me to take Hope back to her bed?"

Lorenzo slowly moved his arms so as not to wake Hope and made room for Sabela to take her from him. "Yes, I am sure you've missed her. It will feel good for you to hold her, yes?"

Sabela managed a weak smile "Yes it will. I'll be right back," she said, with Hope now in her arms.

After she disappeared upstairs, Lorenzo stood and paced the room. "I am so sorry, Slater. I just cannot dishonor Charlotte. She trusts me, and I love her so much. I do not want to lose her trust."

"It's okay, Lorenzo. I understand, and I know Sabela does too. I'm glad we came home so we can talk to Charlotte in the morning. Thank you so much for being here for her and the kids."

Lorenzo smiled. "In the morning I will cook us all a big breakfast, and we can talk around the table. If you want to take Scottie to school, I will fix breakfast while you are gone."

"Sounds good, Lorenzo. Now why don't you go back to bed, Sabela and I are going to try and get some sleep down here."

# CHAPTER 23

## SABELA

olding Hope, I tiptoed into our darkened room, illuminated only by the nightlight next to the twin's cribs. I managed a weak smile when I looked down at Joy sleeping soundly, gently placing Hope in her crib next to Joy as I held my breath and made sure she remained sleeping and didn't stir.

The subtle sound of my mom's breathing was the only sound in the room. I tiptoed to her side of the bed and looked down at her. She looked so peaceful; I had a strong urge to wake her and ask her what was going on, but that would be selfish on my part, so I resisted.

I gently placed my hand on her exposed shoulder and whispered, "I love you, Mom," before turning around and leaving the room.

When I returned downstairs, Slater had already gotten blankets from the linen closet. He'd pulled out one of the hide-a-way beds, and was now in the process of making up the bed.

Slater looked up and smiled as I walked down the stairs. "Hey, how's Hope?"

He took me in his arms and kissed my forehead. "She's fine.

Sleeping soundly, and my mom is too." I rested my head on his chest. "I'm so worried about her. It must be fairly serious if Lorenzo doesn't want to tell us." I looked up and stared into his deep brown eyes. "What could it be?"

Slater rocked me gently in his arms. "I don't know Sabela, but I'm not jumping to any conclusions. We'll find out tomorrow. Until then let's try and get some sleep, okay?"

I nodded and kissed his neck. "You're right. I'm so glad Jill called me and we decided to come home. I know Mom won't be happy, but Jill did the right thing."

As I expected, I had a sleepless night, consumed with worry over my mom, lying awake much of the night and fearing the worst. Finally, at 5:00 am, one of the girls gave me an excuse to get up when I heard one of them fussing from upstairs. I quickly jumped out of bed, surprised to hear Slater's voice.

"Where are you going?" he said, sitting up and revealing his naked chest.

I turned to face him, a look of surprise on my face. "You're awake?"

"I have been for the past hour," he said, turning on the lamp next to the sofa bed and rubbing his eyes.

"Me, too. One of the girls is fussing. I'm going to bring her down and feed her before she wakes Mom."

Slater pulled back the sheets, swung his legs over the side and stood up, wearing only his boxer shorts. "I'll get a bottle ready."

"Thanks. Might as well make it two, the other one should be waking up soon, if not already. I'll be right back," I said, heading upstairs.

The door was ajar to our bedroom, and I quietly tiptoed in and found Lorenzo sitting up, getting ready to get out of bed. I raised my hand and whispered. "I got her. I'll take her downstairs. Let Mom sleep. And if Hope wakes up, I'll come get her. Go back to sleep."

Lorenzo yawned and gave me a sleepy nod. "Thank you."

After retrieving Joy from the crib, Hope began to stir, and I knew it'd be just a matter of minutes before she woke up. I quickly took Joy downstairs and handed her to Slater who was sitting at the kitchen table. "Here, take her, Hope is about to wake up. I'm going to get her."

For the next hour or so Slater and I fed the girls and entertained them until they were ready to take a nap. "I sure have missed them," I said, laying Hope on the fold-out couch.

"Me too," Slater said, laying Joy next to her. "I should go wake up Scottie. He needs to get ready for school."

"He'll sure be surprised to see you," I said with a big smile. "I wonder what time Mom and Lorenzo will come down?"

"I'm sure they're exhausted from watching these three for the past few days, but they'll never tell us that. Let them sleep. They'll come down when they're ready."

Slater returned from taking Scottie to school around 8:30 am. The twins were now awake and playing in their playpen when he walked through the door. He scanned the room. "Charlotte and Lorenzo haven't come down yet?"

I shook my head. "No, but I hear them walking around up there. They should be coming down shortly."

Twenty minutes later as we were sitting on the couch next to the playpen, my mom came down the stairs with Lorenzo close behind. I stood up, walked over to her and gave her a hug. "Hey Mom, I know you're probably upset that we came home early, but I need to know what's going on?"

My mom held me tight, tears pooled in her eyes. "It's okay, Sabela, I'm just so sorry I ruined your honeymoon. I wanted to wait until you got back to tell you."

I pulled back from our embrace and placed my hands on her shoulders. "Mom, please, you did not ruin anything. You're more important than anything else. Now please, tell me what's going on? I couldn't sleep last night I was so worried. Lorenzo wouldn't tell us anything. He said you'd insisted on being the one to tell us. What is it, Mom? I'm really scared."

My mom took my hand and led me to the couch where Slater sat. "Have a seat, Sabela."

My heart raced as I took a seat, my mom then sat down next to me. I took Slater's hand, a lump wedged in my throat, afraid of what she might tell us. Lorenzo followed us into the room and sat in a chair across from us. My mom's eyes filled with tears and her hands shook in her lap. I released my hand from Slater, and with both hands grabbed her hands. "Mom, you're scaring me. Please talk to me. Are you sick?"

My mom squeezed my hands, her voice trembling as she spoke. "Sabela, sweetheart, I have cervical cancer."

# CHAPTER 24

## SABELA

I gasped, tears flowing down my cheeks. My heart sank and fear consumed me. "No! Oh my god, Mom, when did you find out?" I had so many questions. Was it caught early? Will she have surgery? I needed to know.

"I've known for a while, Sabela." She bowed her head and gazed at the floor, avoiding eye contact. "I found out before your wedding."

I was horrified. "What? And you never told me?" More tears fell down my cheeks, my hands shook and my heart raced uncontrollably. "Why, Mom?"

She squeezed my hands again, raised her head and looked into my eyes with sadness. "I couldn't. It would have ruined your wedding, and after a while, I was too scared to tell you, but I've been wanting to, and then when you told me you were taking your honeymoon early, I decided to wait until you came home. I thought I'd be okay watching the kids with Lorenzo helping me and your friends coming by every day, but I'm so tired all the time, and Jill was obviously concerned, which is why she called Claire. Jill has never been able to keep a secret," my mom joked with a weak smile. "I'm so sorry, Sabela, please forgive me. I was just trying to protect you."

My voice shook when I spoke. "It's okay, Mom. So, what's going on now? What stage is it, and are you having any kind of surgery?"

My mom lowered her eyes and looked at our hands entwined, squeezing them tightly. Tears pooled in her eyes, and Slater reached over to the end table, pulling out a tissue from the box and handing it to my mom.

She sniffed and dabbed her eyes. "Thank you." Then she looked at me. "Sabela, sweetheart, there will be no surgery. I have stage four cervical cancer and it has spread to my bones. In September and October I went through five weeks of radiation and chemotherapy, and now I'm taking chemo medication."

Again, I was shocked. "What? How on earth did you keep all of this from me? And why, Mom? I'm your daughter. I should have been there for you."

Tears gushed down my mother's cheeks. I pulled her in and held her tight as she continued to sob. "Sabela, please don't be angry with me. You're here for me now, and seeing you marry Slater and give me two beautiful granddaughters, along with little Scottie, has given me the strength to put up a fight. I want to be around as long as possible and be a part of their lives."

I held my mom tight, allowing my own tears to fall. "But you should have told me, Mom."

My mom pulled back and looked me in the eyes. "How could I? You were experiencing the happiest time of your life. You had just gotten married and gave birth to two beautiful girls. I was not about to crush the happiness you and Slater were experiencing. I couldn't do that to you both." She smiled over at Lorenzo, still sitting on the couch with misty eyes. "Lorenzo has been taking care of me and getting me to my appointments. I'm sorry I didn't tell you sooner, but you must remember, this is my battle, not yours, and I'm doing everything my doctors recommend, but the treatments have left me tired and weak at times." She ran her hands through her hair. "And my hair is much thinner."

Slater spoke next and rested his hand on my shoulder. "I'm sure this is going through Sabela's mind because it's going through mine and I'm sure she's afraid to ask." He paused. "Can you beat this thing? Please tell us you can."

Still embracing my mom, my body froze and I held my breath, waiting for my mom's reply.

"It's in my bones. I will always have cancer, now it's just a matter of trying to keep it from spreading and taking it one day at a time," she explained.

Slater hesitated before he spoke. "We need to know, Charlotte. What is the life expectancy with your condition?"

My mom remained silent and dabbed her eyes again. I pulled back and took her hands in mine. "Mom?"

"It can vary, depending on the progression of the cancer. I've been told one to three years." She squeezed my hands again and took me in her arms. "And I want to make every day count."

I gasped. "Oh, Mom. Surely there's something we can do?"

My mom wept as she spoke. "I'm doing it, Sabela. I'm surrounded by family and I'm okay with everything. I've accepted my diagnoses and will doing everything in my power to remain positive and take care of myself for as long as I can."

"We're here for you, Mom; I still wished you'd told us sooner, but from now on, anything you need, we're here for you."

My mom released a small laugh. "Sabela, honey, you have your hands full with the twins and Scottie. I don't want you to feel sorry for me. Most days I'm feeling good, but occasionally the fatigue catches up with me. Lorenzo knows this, and on those days he just lets me sleep."

I continued to sob. "I don't want you to die, Mom."

"None of us are getting out of this alive, Sabela. Let's not dwell on what time I may have left. Today is a good day. I'm feeling good and I want to enjoy it with you, Slater, Lorenzo and the twins, and when Scottie comes home from school, I'd like us all to go to the park for a picnic." She smiled. "Can we do that?"

I nodded and forced a smile through my tears. "Yes, Mom, we can do that."

Lorenzo kept his promise and made us all a big breakfast consisting of eggs, pancakes, sausage and bacon, while my mom and I entertained the twins, and Slater called his boss Joseph to let him know we were back in town.

After my mom had broken the devastating news to us, the one-on-one time with her and the girls suddenly took on a whole different meaning. I was no longer taking our time for granted and was cherishing every minute we spent together, wondering how many moments like this I'd have with her. I kept pausing and looking at my mom with misty eyes, knowing her days were numbered. I wanted more days like this. I smiled when she picked up Hope, kissed her on the cheek and cradled her in her arms. I knew what I wanted to do and needed to share my thoughts with Slater before suggesting the idea to Mom and Lorenzo.

An hour later Slater came downstairs, smiling after ending his call with Joseph.

I looked up as I sat on the living room floor with Joy. "How did it go?"

His smile grew. "Great! Ricky and I are meeting with him tomorrow to go over the contracts and plans and discuss a starting date. I told him we still have some small jobs to wrap up and won't schedule anymore." He smiled again. "Looks like we'll be hiring an extensive crew, too. I still can't believe this is happening," he said, walking over to me and taking Joy into his arms.

I stood up and wrapped my arms around his waist, smiling at Joy as she looked up at her dad with her big brown eyes. "That's fantastic, I'm so proud of you!"

My mom looked at Hope in her arms and kissed her nose. "Did you hear that, Hope? Daddy has a new job, and it's a good one." She looked at us standing in the middle of the room and embraced us both in her arms and smiled. "I'm so happy for you two. You've worked so hard growing your business, and it's finally paying off. I love you both so much."

"We love you too, Mom, and as soon as Lorenzo is out of the shower we're going to spend the entire day together and go to the park."

# CHAPTER 25

## SLATER

Spending the day at the park with Charlotte and Lorenzo was just what we needed. Quality family time that at times were emotional with heartfelt conversations about Charlotte's diagnoses and being strong for her, even though our hearts were ripping apart.

Claire and Jill had both texted Sabela during the day while we were at the park, and Sabela had told me before replying that she didn't want to give them the news about her mom via text or a phone call, but instead insisted on telling them in person. I agreed, and she texted them back, telling them we were spending the day with her mom and Lorenzo and would see them tomorrow. When Claire texted back asking how her mom was, Sabela replied, avoiding the question, and texted back. 'She's playing with Hope, I gotta go, I'll see you tomorrow.' That seemed to satisfy Claire's curiosity because she never texted back.

When I left to go pick up Scottie from school, I used the idle time driving alone in my truck to call Dwayne. He answered on the second ring. "Hey, Slater, good to hear from you. How's Sabela's mom?"

I paused. "Not good, I'm afraid. She has cervical cancer that's spread to her bones. We're still in shock over the news, doing our best to be strong for her, but it's not easy."

"Oh, Slater, I have you on speaker, Tammy's here, and we're both so sorry to hear that. Is there anything we can do?"

"Thanks, man. You guys have already done so much for us. We're just taking it one day at a time. Still letting it soak in and trying to be there for Lorenzo and Charlotte. But I also wanted to tell you that this doesn't change our dinner plans for next week. We must keep living. We're excited to have you meet what we call our best friends and extended family. I hope you can still make it."

"Yes, of course. We're looking forward to it," Dwayne replied.

"Great! Sabela still needs to talk to Claire about it, because we'd like to have dinner at her and Travis' house. It's the biggest," I laughed. "Sabela is seeing her tomorrow, and I'm sure she'll love the idea. Claire loves to entertain," I chuckled. "I'll call you in a day or so with the details and address."

"Sounds good, and again, we're so sorry to hear about Sabela's mom; give Sabela our love."

"I sure will, and thanks, guys."

When we returned home from the park in two cars (our SUV was still at the terminal and we'd had to take my truck and Lorenzo's car), I spent some time in the office getting my documents in order for my meeting with Joseph. I also called Ricky, who said he would give me a ride to pick up our car at the ferry terminal after our meeting. Charlotte retired to her room for a nap, while Sabela and Lorenzo fixed dinner and Scottie entertained his sisters.

Later that night, lying on the sofa bed with Sabela in my arms, thoughts of the day and Charlotte were going through my mind. Sabela squeezed my waist and kissed my chest. "I love you so much, Slater. I don't ever want to lose you."

I kissed the top of her head. "I'm not going anywhere. I love you too, sweetheart."

"It scares me, not knowing how long I have with my mom. I

want to be around her every second and every minute of the day. I don't want her to go home tomorrow," Sable confessed.

"She won't be that far away, sweetheart. It's a thirty minute drive." I squeezed her shoulder. "We can go see her whenever we want to."

Sabela released a heavy sigh. "We both know how that goes. When was the last time I drove to my mom's? We're always so busy with work and the kids. Slater, she's hidden her cancer and treatment from me for months. I was angry and hurt at first that she'd shut me out and kept it from me, but I understand why, and it also made me realize how much I've not been a part of her life sometimes. I want to be there for her every single day, and I want the kids to know and remember her, not as someone they just see occasionally. I want them to have fond memories of her and cherish them."

I sensed she was leading up to something. "What are you trying to say, Sabela?"

Sabela lifted her head and looked me in the eyes. I want Mom and Lorenzo to move in with us. This must be hard on Lorenzo, too. I don't want him to care for my mom on his own. He's no spring chicken either, and I'm sure he gets tired, but he's being strong for her, and I doubt he ever complains, or even confesses how hard this must be on him."

I was stunned by Sabela's wishes, but at the same time understood her concerns, and, in fact, agreed with her. "You're right, this must be truly difficult for Lorenzo and it's only right we'd be there for the two of them. Have you talked to your mom about this?"

Sabela shook her head. "No, I wanted to talk to you first. I learnt my lesson making a triple wedding plan before talking to you," she chuckled. "What do you think? I mean we've been talking about looking for a bigger house. Let's look for one that will accommodate Lorenzo and my mom, too."

I smiled and hugged her. "I love the idea."

Sabela's eyes grew wide. "You do?"

I smiled, again. "Yes, I do. I think it's a wonderful idea, but I think we should talk to your mom first and see what she has to say before we go looking for a bigger house."

Sabela nodded. "Yes, I agree. I plan on talking to her tomorrow while you're in your meeting. In the meantime, how do you feel about sleeping on this sofa bed for a while until we've found a house? I don't want my mom to go home. I want her to stay here."

I laughed. "I'm fine with it, but again, let's see what your mom feels about the idea before committing to a sofa bed and looking for a house big enough for four adults and three kids."

Sabela gave my middle a squeeze. "Okay, but I think she'll like the idea. Good night. I love you."

"I love you too," I replied with a loving smile, turning off the lamp next to the sofa bed.

The next morning Sabela and Lorenzo took care of the girls, feeding and dressing them, allowing Charlotte to sleep in. I think she was fatigued from our day at the park yesterday. I showered and got dressed for my meeting. By 7:30 am Sabela had Scottie dressed and ready for school so I could drop him off before meeting up with Ricky.

Once I was back in the morning traffic after dropping Scottie off, my mind began to wander back to my conversation with Sabela last night. As much as I liked her idea, I couldn't help feeling a bit of sadness when it came to letting go of my dreams of living on Catalina Island. I honestly pictured my family and I living and raising our kids there. It was the perfect location, and a dream I had not given up on until now. I hadn't managed to sell Sabela on the idea. I don't think she knew how serious I was about it, but I definitely was. But with Charlotte's diagnoses, I needed to think of Charlotte and her needs, and that we needed to be there for her.

My thoughts reminded me to ask Joseph if he'd had a chance to see if there were any homes for sale in the area. I made a mental note to bring it up in our meeting.

# CHAPTER 26

## SABELA

*I* had yet another restless sleep last night, tossing and turning and thinking about my mom and the fact that she has cancer. She didn't use the word, but as much as my heart ached at the thought, there is no cure; it's terminal. It has spread to her bones, and it's just a matter of time before the cancer will win and steal her away from me. Not knowing how long I'll have her in my life is what kept me awake. Suddenly it felt like the clock was ticking. It could be a few months or a few years. No matter what precious time we have together, I wanted every second to count. As soon as she comes downstairs, I'm going to talk to her about my idea. I think she'll be pleased and will love it.

I gave Slater a kiss on the lips before he left with Scottie. He looked tired, and I knew my tossing and turning had disrupted his sleep, and a wave of guilt swept through me. He needed to be rested and fresh for his meeting. It was the most important day of his career, and our future depended on it.

"Are you okay?" I asked, pulling away from our kiss.

He nodded and smiled as he held Scottie's hand and his backpack in the other. "Yeah, I'm okay. What about you, though? I heard you get up twice last night and go into the kitchen."

"I'm okay. My mom is constantly on my mind. I'm going to talk to her today about her moving in with us."

"Great, I think she'll go for it. Don't forget to talk to Claire about Dwayne and Tammy coming for dinner. I want the whole gang to be there, and Claire has the space."

"I'm calling her today and will probably go over there with my mom."

We kissed again and I held the door open as he and Scottie walked over to the truck. I smiled and waved as Slater backed out onto the main road.

While the twins slept soundly in the playpen, I managed to take a quick shower and get dressed in jeans and a black t-shirt. When I returned downstairs, my hair damp and a towel draped around my neck, I found my mom sitting on the couch looking down at the twins who were still sleeping.

"They sure are beautiful," she said, wearing a sweet smile.

I joined her on the couch and rubbed her shoulder. "They sure are. I think Hope has Dad's eyes."

"I'll have to take a closer look when they're open," my mom said, smiling.

I rubbed her shoulder again. "How are you feeling?"

She released a heavy sigh and leaned back against the cushions of the couch. "I'm doing okay. I think today is going to be a good day, which is great, because Lorenzo and I need to pack and get back home so you can have your bedroom back. He's resting right now. When he comes downstairs, we'll start packing."

I paused before speaking. "I wanted to talk to you about that, Mom. Obviously, this has been hard on Lorenzo, too, taking you for your treatments and appointments, along with taking care of you."

My mom nodded. "It might be, but he never complains."

"And I don't think he ever will, Mom, which is why I have an idea."

"You do? What's that Sabela?" my mom asked, smiling.

"I talked to Slater last night and he liked what I said." I squeezed her hand. "We'd like you and Lorenzo to come live with us, Mom. We want to help you and make it easier on both of you. What do you say?" I asked eagerly, grinning.

My mom's jaw dropped. "Oh Sabela, I don't know. What about my house?" She looked around the room. "This place is not big enough for all of us and you can't keep sleeping on the sofa bed."

I wasn't expecting my mom to question my invitation and tried to convince her it was a good idea. "We've already been thinking about buying a bigger house, Mom. You know that, and we can look for one that'll be big enough for all of us. You'll get to see the twins and Scottie every day. Lorenzo will have help, and we can all be a family under one roof."

"Oh Sabela, I don't know what to say. I'd have to talk it over with Lorenzo. It concerns him, and neither one of us wants to be a burden to you or Slater."

"You're my mom, you could never be a burden to me. I want to be there for you. You wouldn't let me be there when you first discovered you had cancer; let me be there now. Please Mom, don't shut me out again."

"I do like the idea of seeing you and the kids every day. I do miss you all when I'm at my house, and neither Lorenzo or I like to drive much anymore," my mom confessed.

"I miss you too, and I've been so busy with the girls and running the administrative part of our business that I've not visited you as much as I should have. I feel terrible about that, especially with what you've been going through."

My mom gave me a hard stare. "Now Sabela, you take that back. You have nothing to feel guilty about. I was the one that decided not to tell you, and I explained my reasons. You have your life here with your beautiful family. You can't be everywhere, Sabela. The kids need you, so does Slater."

I let out a big sigh. "And so do you Mom, which is why I want you to move in with us. Just tell Lorenzo you want to, and I know he'll agree to anything you'd like to do."

My mom smiled. "You have it all figured out, don't you? Give me a few days at home alone with Lorenzo and I'll talk to him, okay?"

I was saddened that I didn't get a yes, but understood she needed to discuss my idea with Lorenzo. "Okay Mom, but if it's the house you're worried about, we can help you pack and move."

My mom cracked a laugh. "If it happens, I'm definitely holding you to that. I know it will be too much for Lorenzo and I."

I patted my mom's knee. "Okay, why don't I go make us some coffee while you sit here and watch the girls. Lorenzo should be coming down soon, and I want to call Claire this morning, and go over and discuss the dinner party we want to have with our new friends Dwayne and Tammy that I told you about," I said, walking to the kitchen.

"They sound wonderful. That was so nice of them to give you a ride on their boat to San Diego Harbor. I can't wait to meet them."

I filled the coffee pot with water as I spoke, occasionally looking over my shoulder at my mom. "Well, I want the entire gang to be there for dinner. They're looking forward to meeting all of you. In fact, I want you to come to Claire's today and be a part of the planning if that's okay with you? You always have such good ideas. Remember, it was your idea to have the tri-colored wedding. That was brilliant," I laughed. "Or as Jill called it, The Lucky Charms Wedding."

My mom matched my laugh. "We would love to go with you, but what about packing?"

I waved my hands. "Don't worry about it. Spend another night here," I said, turning on the coffee pot and grabbing three cups from the cupboard.

My mom smiled. "Okay, we can do that if Lorenzo doesn't mind."

# CHAPTER 27

## SABELA

*L*orenzo agreed to spend another night and seemed pleased that he wouldn't have to spend the morning packing. I decided not to mention my idea to him about having them move in with us. My mom made it clear she wanted to talk to him alone in her own home.

Mom and Lorenzo offered to feed the girls while I escaped to the office for a few minutes to call Claire.

"Hey Sabela, I've been so worried about your mom. How is she?"

I didn't want to tell her over the phone about my mom's cancer, so I made my reply short and quickly changed the subject. "She's doing okay. I'll tell you more when I see you. Do you mind if we come over today? I want to talk to you about a dinner party."

"A dinner party? Where?" Claire asked.

"At your house," I said with a smirk.

"Well, technically it's you and Slater's house," Claire joked.

"Oh stop it, Claire. It will always be a home for the children and you guys. You both know that."

"I know. I'm just messing with you. But sure, come on over.

Jill's here and we'd love to see those beautiful girls of yours. Then you can tell me all about this dinner party I'm apparently having."

I laughed at her sarcasm. "We'll be there in a few hours. Say hi to Jill," I said.

***

By 11:00 am Hope and Joy were strapped into their car seats in the back seat of Lorenzo's car, also an SUV, as mine was still at the terminal. My mom sat in the front and Lorenzo took the second back seat, allowing me to drive. I still hadn't heard from Slater and persuaded myself not to call him. I knew he would call me the first chance he got to let me know how everything was going.

I checked the time as I pulled out of the driveway and calculated that I had just over three hours before I'd have to leave Claire's to pick up Scottie from school. That was plenty of time to discuss everything with Claire, visit with the children and everyone else.

When we arrived, I parked on the street in front of the house. Lorenzo took Hope as I picked up Joy from her car seat. My mom waited on the curb next to the car. The girls were both wide awake, smiling and gazing down the street as we walked up to the large, wooden front door. After ringing the bell, Jill opened the door dressed in jeans and a pink sweater, greeting us with a large grin.

"Hey guys, come on in. It's so good to see you," she said, pinching Joy's cheek as I entered and walked by her. Joy laughed as Jill looked at me with pleading eyes. "Can I hold her?"

"Of course," I replied. "She's getting big. My arm is getting tired."

Jill anxiously took Joy and nestled her arms around her. Joy instantly relaxed in her arms and began tugging Jill's hair. I was still surprised how natural and warm Jill was with kids. One day she would make a brilliant mom I told myself, following her into the front room. I looked around the empty room. "Where is everyone?" I asked.

"The children are in class right now. They'll be breaking for lunch in half an hour. Caroline, Travis' mom, is aiding in the classes, and Claire's mom, Abigail, is reading outside and watching the dogs," Jill said.

"That's so cool you're able to bring your dog Maggie to work with you every day." I looked out the double French doors and laughed at Tilly, Claire's little Yorkshire Terrier, chasing Jill's larger dog, a Golden Retriever, around on the grass. "They sure get along."

"Oh, they're inseparable when I'm here. I swear, I hate pulling them apart when I have to go home. I almost feel guilty."

"Where's Claire?" I asked, walking away from the French doors and over to Lorenzo who still carried Hope.

"She's in her office. I'll let her know you're here after I've put Joy in the playpen." She looked over at my mom standing in the room. "Charlotte, why don't you have a seat on the couch, and I'll get us all some iced lemonade in a few minutes."

I took Hope from Lorenzo and followed Jill over to the playpen where we placed both girls and watched them for a few minutes as they each picked up a plush toy and explored it with their mouths.

"I'll be right back," Jill said. "Make yourselves at home."

I stood in the middle of the room as my mom and Lorenzo took a seat on the couch, admiring the pictures on the walls of all six foster children who lived in the home with Claire and Travis. The pictures had been taken on the grass in the backyard, and I smiled when I saw how happy they all looked. In the short time they'd been here, Claire and Travis had done an amazing job of making this a home for the children where they could feel safe and loved.

The transition has been amazing, and with the help of Jill, who had an immediate special bond with Jasmine, and Claire's and Travis' moms, they had created a wonderful family environment for six children who'd been swallowed up in the terrible foster system. Six children were the maximum they could house, and now with Claire pregnant with their first child, they were at full capacity.

If Claire and Travis could take more, they would have in a heartbeat. They were also adamant that the six children that they'd grown to love would be their responsibility, even to adulthood if necessary, until they found a family which they'd personally approved of. Neither of them would allow any of their children to go through the horrors Travis had experienced; shuffled from foster home to foster home until he was sixteen, then finally run away.

Yes, Claire was correct, we did own the house. Slater inherited it after Eve, Scottie's biological mother, died. We chose not to live in it and instead turned it into a children's home. It was one of the best decisions we'd ever made.

A few minutes later Claire walked into the room followed by Jill.

I smiled. Her pregnancy bump was beginning to show a little, and she rubbed her stomach as she greeted us. "Hey Sabela." She turned and looked over at Charlotte sitting on the couch. "Hi Charlotte, glad to see you're feeling better."

I avoided her comment and leaned in to give her a hug. "Hi Claire, you look radiant. Pregnancy certainly agrees with you. How's everything going?"

She took a seat on the other empty couch, and I sat down next to her. Jill knelt by the playpen and started baby talking to Joy and Hope. They both laughed instantaneously.

"The pregnancy is going really well," she smiled. "I'm feeling great, watching my diet, and Travis keeps me in check," she laughed, "making sure I don't do too much." She turned and smiled at Jill. "Jill's been fantastic, and mine and Travis' mom have been a tremendous help. Just a few more weeks and I'll be past the first trimester, then I'll likely be able to relax a bit."

"I'm sure you'll be fine," I reassured her.

Claire leaned back on the couch, her hand on her belly. "What about you? I can't believe you got stung by a bat ray! When Slater told me that you had a severe allergic reaction, we all got really scared."

"I'm doing fine, and my mom told me the same thing happened to my dad before I was born. I had no idea."

"Oh, wow!" She looked over at my mom and smiled. "And you're feeling better, Charlotte?"

Lorenzo took her hand and squeezed it before she spoke. "I'm okay Claire, thank you."

Being the inquisitive one, Claire asked more questions. "Were you sick from something you ate?"

I felt the need to save my mom from an uncomfortable conversation and butted in. "Claire, Jill, my mom has cervical cancer."

Claire's jaw dropped, Jill stood up and put her hand over her gaping mouth. "Oh no! I'm so sorry," Claire said, pity in her eyes.

There was fear in Jill's eyes as she spoke. "What is your doctor going to do?"

For the next twenty minutes, Claire and Jill listened in silence. I repeated the conversation I had with my mom the previous day. Just like Slater and I, they were shocked to learn that my mom had hidden her diagnoses from us before the wedding. After I finished telling them the news, Claire spoke up first.

"I don't know what to say. Are you sure there's nothing they can do?"

I shook my head. "They've done all they can. It's in her bones. She's on chemo meds right now, and we're hoping that it'll slow down the cancer."

Jill picked up Hope who was fussing, smiling at my mom, and

spoke softly. "We're here for you. Anything you need, please let us know."

Claire's ears pricked up. "I hear footsteps upstairs which means the kids must be breaking for lunch." She patted my thigh. "Let's eat and visit with them, and when they go back to class, we can discuss this dinner party I'm supposedly having. Travis should be back from Home Depot by then, and I'm sure he'll want to hear about it too," she laughed.

# CHAPTER 28

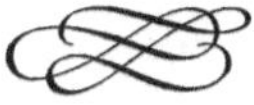

## SLATER

Ricky texted me five minutes from my destination to let me know he was standing outside the building of Joseph's office. After parking my truck in the underground parking lot, I walked out to the front and spotted Ricky talking on the phone. I was immediately impressed with his attire consisting of black jeans and a black shirt.

I knew when he ended his call with 'I love you too, babe,' that he was talking to Jill. "Hey man, you clean up pretty well. How's Jill?" I asked, giving him a friendly pat on the shoulder.

Ricky looked down at his wardrobe and smiled. "Thanks man, you do too. Must say though, I feel like a stiff; I prefer my relaxed jeans and a t-shirt."

"I hear you," I laughed. "How's Jill?" I asked again.

"She's fine, loving her work and being with the kids. Her and Jasmine went for a morning walk before classes started and she told me that Sabela and her mom are going over there today."

"Yeah, after we pick up my car from the ferry terminal I'd like to meet them over there. We want to do a dinner party there and you're invited."

"Great man! What's the party for?" Ricky asked, rubbing his hands together, anticipating a fun time.

"Well, before I tell you, let's see if Claire agrees to having it at her place first." I shifted the folder wedged under my arm. "Okay, we ready to go in?"

"Sure am, boss. Let's do this," Ricky said, smiling.

I was surprised how relaxed I was riding in the elevator and walking down the hallway to Joseph's office. I thought for sure I'd be a bundle of nerves, but after talking to him on the phone from Catalina Island, his mannerisms and business ethics instantly put me at ease. He's been in the industry for years, and I'm sure he's done hundreds of these deals and meetings. He knew exactly what to say to build my confidence, and showed nothing but enthusiasm to have the opportunity to work with us. I can certainly see why he's the top guy. You can't help but like him.

He greeted us with a big friendly smile and a firm handshake, making us feel welcome. He then offered us coffee and pastries as soon as we took a seat at the conference table, which already had plans laid out, as well as a screen with slides of the development.

The meeting lasted roughly three hours. It was decided we should increase our crew by fifty percent, with Ricky overseeing the hiring. Outside contractors would be hired to do the electrical, plumbing and interior. We would oversee the structural, which included the roofing and foundation. Joseph estimated that all of the permits should be in place by mid-February, so a start date was set for the second week of March, just four months away.

After our initial meeting was over, I was surprised when Joseph brought up the subject of us looking to buy a house before I did.

"Hey Slater, I wanted to let you know that I've not had a chance to look at the real estate market yet for a house for you and your family, but now that we have this meeting behind us, I should have a little free time; I'll do some checking around for you."

I nodded. "Thanks, I appreciate it. We may be having my

mother-in-law and her boyfriend live with us too, so we might need another room," I told him.

Joseph patted his desk with the palm of his hand. "No problem. I'll let you know what I find."

After signing the necessary papers and confirming our next conference meeting via a Zoom call, Ricky and I left feeling pleased with the achievements of the meeting. Once in the elevator, Ricky looked at me with concern.

"Charlotte might be moving in with you? Is she okay?"

I paused before replying, wondering if it was my place to break the sad news. I then realized that by the time we arrived at Claire's place, Sabela and Charlotte would have already told the others, so I decided to break the news to Ricky. "Charlotte has cancer, and it's not good I'm afraid."

"Oh no. I'm so sorry. How bad is it?"

"She has cervical cancer stage four which has spread to her bones."

"Jesus - how is Sabela taking it?"

"She's trying to be strong for her mom, but on the inside she's torn up and devastated of course, just as I am, but what surprised us was that she's known about the cancer since before the wedding. With so much going on with the birth of the twins and the wedding, she didn't want to be that dark cloud raining on our happy events. I can't say I blame her, but she went through treatment and everything, and we had no idea."

Ricky's tone dropped a notch. "Icy, is that why you two want a dinner party? Is it some sort of final farewell to Charlotte? Seems pretty depressing to me, man."

I shook my head. "No, man. We have no idea how long Charlotte has, could be a few months, or hopefully a few years, which is why Sabela suggested she and Lorenzo move in with us. She wants to be with her mom as much as possible and have her around the kids. The dinner has nothing to do with Charlotte."

"Okay, well now I want to get over to Claire's and find out what this dinner feast is all about."

I looked at my phone and saw it was almost noon. "Let me call Sabela and make sure they're still there. We still have to drop off my truck at my house and go pick up my SUV from the ferry terminal before heading over there. Ricky waited patiently as I made the call. I smiled when Sabela's beautiful voice came on the phone.

"Hey babe, how'd it go?" she asked.

"Fantastic, it couldn't have gone any better! We're all done, so if you're still at Claire's we can head over there after picking up the SUV."

"Yep, we're here. The kids are still in class.When they break for lunch, we're going to visit with them, then when they return to class we can talk to Claire and everyone about the dinner."

"Sounds good, we'll be there as soon as we can. Oh, and Sabela,"
"Yes?"

I paused. "I told Ricky about your mom. I hope I didn't over-step any boundaries, but the subject of your mom moving in with us came up and I didn't want to lie to him."

"It's okay. I'm glad you did. I also told Jill and Claire, and I'll tell the others when the kids are in class."

"Okay, I love you. See you soon."

# CHAPTER 29

## SABELA

*I* was relieved Slater had told Ricky about my mom, that way he had time to process it before coming over.

Deep in thought later in the day, I was suddenly ambushed by the two youngest foster kids; Colin and Matthew, both three years old, soon to be four next month. Both held up a painting, looking proud of their achievements.

"Sabela, look what I painted!" Colin shouted as he ran into my space and hugged my waist.

Matthew followed closely behind. "I painted a tiger," he yelled, his little face glowing with pride.

I knelt to the level of both boys, took their artwork, and admired them with a huge smile. "They are amazing! Can I hang them on the wall in the kitchen?"

Colin and Matthew eagerly nodded and led me to the space in the kitchen dedicated to the children's artwork.

Claire's mom Abigail soon joined us from outside. After greeting me with a hug, I set forth to fix lunch for the kids. I offered to help make peanut butter and jelly sandwiches and fresh fruit salads. I laughed when the rest of the kids, Kate, Nicole,

Jasmine and Janet, came racing down the stairs and surrounded Jill with hugs, still sitting by the playpen where the twins were playing.

Overwhelmed with her space being ambushed, Jill stood up laughing and yelled across the room, "I'm taking this lot outside to play with Tilly and Maggie until lunch is ready. Charlotte and Lorenzo can watch the girls with Claire."

I watched with a full heart as Jill's little army of admirers followed her outside, all wanting to hold her hand.

"Wow! The kids sure love her," I said, adding jelly to the rows of sliced bread on the counter.

"They sure do," Abigail replied, cutting up a watermelon. "She's a natural."

I stared out the kitchen window, watching the kids and Jill race around the grass playing catch with the dogs. "What a beautiful family," I said with a full heart. "We've done pretty well saving these kids from the system; our hard work seems like it's finally paid off."

"It sure has," I heard Slater whisper in my ear as he slid his hands around my waist and kissed my neck.

I jumped and laughed at the same time. "You startled me! I didn't hear you come in."

"Caroline let us in, we just got here," Slater said, as he swayed my body wrapped in his arms and nuzzled his chin on my shoulder.

I squeezed his forearms as he held me tight, nestling my head against his. "I'm so happy to hear the meeting went well."

He released his hold and spun me around. I giggled as he kissed me passionately on the lips. "It went better than well. It was fantastic. Joseph is a real pro when it comes to these developments. I still can't believe he hired me."

"Hey now, don't say that. You're good at what you do, and obviously Joseph knows that too. You deserve this job as much as the next guy." I kissed him on the lips. "Let me grab you a beer from the fridge, you need to celebrate. Does Ricky want one?"

"Better ask him, he went out to see Jill as soon as we got here."

I looked outside and saw Ricky joining in a game of tag with the children. "They need to have a kid of their own. They'd be amazing parents," I said, smiling.

"I think they're still playing and enjoying life being just the two of them. Neither one of them has shown a desire to have a kid anytime soon," Slater noted.

"Well, one day a kid is going to be super lucky to have those two for parents."

As I was finishing up making the sandwiches and putting them on paper plates, I heard the front door open and close. A few seconds later Travis walked into the room. "Travis!" I said with a huge smile. "How was Home Depot?"

Travis smiled and immediately walked over to Claire who was in the living room with Lorenzo and Abigail. "How are you doing, wifey?" he asked, sitting down next to her and putting his arm around her shoulders.

"I'm good." She patted his knee. "And don't worry, I've been a good girl, sitting here visiting with Sabela's mom and watching the twins fall asleep."

Travis kissed her forehead and came into the kitchen as I was putting the last sandwich on a plate. "Good to see you, Sabela. I'm sorry you had to cut your honeymoon short, but your mom looks like she's doing better."

It suddenly dawned on me that Travis didn't know about my mom's cancer. I leaned in and whispered in his ear. "She has cancer, Travis. But please, let's not talk to my mom about it."

His jaw dropped and he pulled back, then leaned in to whisper in my ear. "Shit, Sabela."

I whispered again. "Mom doesn't like to talk about it. I'll tell you more later."

He nodded and whispered. "Okay."

My voice returned to normal when I spoke again. "Okay, lunch is ready. Can you round everyone up while Abigail and I set the table?"

An hour later the children's bellies were full, and right on time, their teacher, Helen Hash, returned from her lunch. Claire had told me that she was quiet, kept to herself and left every day to have lunch with her boyfriend. After class resumed and we were left with a quiet room, two tired dogs sleeping in the yard and twins napping in the playpen, I thought that it would be the perfect time to discuss the dinner party. The only one missing was Caroline who was aiding in the classes, but I figured Claire could fill her in later.

"Okay everyone, let's gather around the table and discuss the dinner party while Hope and Joy are sleeping," I announced to everyone in the room.

"Coming," Jill said, pulling herself away from Ricky where they'd been snuggling on the couch. She stood up, took his hand and pulled him to his feet.

Slater took a seat next to me followed by Claire and Travis. Close behind were Ricky and Jill. Ricky tickled Jill's waist as he walked behind her, causing her to giggle. My mom, Lorenzo and Abigail were the last to join us, carrying glasses and a cold pitcher of lemonade.

"Okay Sabela, I've been dying to know about this dinner party that Travis and I are supposedly having," Claire said, pouring herself a glass of lemonade.

I looked at Slater, patted his knee and smiled. "Why don't you tell them, honey."

Slater leaned back in his chair and smiled. "As you all know, Sabela was stung by a bat ray on the beach of Catalina Island and had a serious allergic reaction to the poison. She went into anaphylactic shock and had to be hospitalized overnight. When it happened, I was really scared and had no idea what to do, and I will be forever grateful to a wonderful couple that helped me when Sabela went into shock and couldn't breathe." Slater folded his arms as he continued with the story. "Growing up around the ocean and being a commercial fisherman, Dwayne knew exactly what to do, and his wife is now an author, but she also fished with her husband. They assisted us in getting Sabela the help she needed, and quickly, I might add. When we heard that Charlotte was not feeling well, Sabela wanted nothing more than to come home. Dwayne and Tammy went out of their way and took us to San Diego Harbor on their boat in the middle of the night. Sabela and I would love for all of you to meet them, and we've invited them over for dinner next weekend." Slater released a chuckle. "Well, after we'd asked them, we soon realized that our place was too small to host such a large dinner, and, well, Claire and Travis, this amazing home immediately popped into our heads."

Claire matched his chuckle. "We'd love to meet them."

Everyone around the table nodded and echoed Claire's words.

"I think having them here would be perfect," Claire added.

I joined in on the conversation. "We've told them all about the home, and the foster kids, and how long we've all been friends and are practically family. They have a home in the mountains out of LA and a small cottage on Catalina Island."

"And their boat is amazing!" Slater added. "Dwayne even said he'd take us all fishing one day."

"That'd be awesome," Travis said, his eyes bright. "I used to love fishing. I've not done it in years, and I've never been ocean fishing. Just freshwater in streams and lakes."

"I don't want you guys doing all the cooking," I insisted. "This is our idea, and I'll take care of all the food and beverages."

Claire raised her hand and grinned. "Fine by me."

"I'd be happy to help," Abigail said.

"Thanks, Abigail. Some of the meals you've made here have been amazing. Do you have any idea what we should fix?"

"How about a big pot of spaghetti, garlic bread and a salad?

Easy to fix, and the kids love spaghetti, so they can eat it too," Abigail suggested.

I grinned. "Sounds perfect. Slater and I will buy everything this week. Saturday we can come over early with all the fixings, and, with your help, cook it up in no time."

"Are you going to invite Sadie and Logan?" Jill asked.

"Yes, I'll call them tomorrow," I replied.

"This should be fun," Claire said, taking a sip of her beverage. "They sound like our kind of people."

Slater smiled. "We know you'll like them, and Sabela and I are excited for you to meet them. "

I matched Slater's smile. "We only hang out with the best, which is why we love you guys," I said, raising my glass.

# CHAPTER 30

## SABELA

It's been three days since my mom and Lorenzo went back home, and I haven't been able to relax ever since. I find myself consumed with worry and just want to be with her 24/7. I want to take care of her and be there, not only for her, but Lorenzo, too. I tried to talk her into staying for a few more days, but she insisted on leaving, explaining that she needed to discuss her options with Lorenzo. Even though I wasn't happy with her decision I had to respect it, and with tears in my eyes, I walked her out to Lorenzo's car, carrying her luggage. I waved as they drove away. I stood at the end of the driveway, tears streaming down my face until I could no longer see them.

I'm not sure how many times a day I've called since they'd left, but I know it's been a lot. I can't take my mind off of her and the fact that she has cancer, and that our days as mother and daughter are numbered rips at my heart.

Slater has been my rock over the past few days, holding me in his arms until I fall asleep at night, playing with me and the kids after a long day at work, trying to distract me from depressing thoughts. If it wasn't for him and the kids, I don't know how I would have handled this.

On the third day of my mom being gone and still no word on whether she would move in with us, I decided to call her after Slater left for work and ask her again. I hadn't brought it up since she'd left. As she'd requested, she needed time to think about it. But I was growing impatient and was anxious to hear her agree that she'd come live with us. I knew I was being self-ish, but my mom can be stubborn at times and has a lot of pride. She proved that by not sharing her diagnoses with us. Maybe she just needs a little push from me to come to a decision?

With Joy in my arms who was now holding her own bottle, I sat on the couch next to the playpen where Hope held her bottle. I called my mom. After three rings, she answered.

She had caller ID on her landline and knew it was me. "Hi Sabela. Everything okay?"

Typical of my mom, always thinking of others before herself. "Everything is fine, Mom. I'm just calling to see how you're doing?"

"I'm just as good as I was when you called last night before you went to bed. There's no need to call me five or six times throughout the day, Sabela. We're fine. We're going out for lunch today at a new Italian restaurant Lorenzo's been dying to try."

"I just worry about you Mom, and I miss you being here. I loved seeing you every day and watching you play with the girls." I knew I was projecting a guilt trip on her, but I couldn't help myself.

"I miss my girls. Give them a big kiss from Grandma."

"I will, Mom." I paused, hesitating to ask what had been on my mind since she'd left. "Mom."

"Yes, Sabela?"

"Have you thought any more about moving in with us? Slater and I still love the idea, and you'd see the girls every day."

"Honey, I'm still thinking about it. I've not made up my mind yet."

"Have you talked to Lorenzo about it? What did he say?"

This time my Mom paused. "I have not, Sabela. I need some time to think it over myself before talking to him."

I was surprised by her reply. "Oh, you haven't? I thought you'd have brought it up as soon as you were home."

"It's a lot to think about, sweetheart. I've lived in this house for decades with your father before he passed, and it holds so many wonderful memories."

I was crushed by what she said but understood completely. How could I have been so selfish? I was asking her to do a lot more than simply move in with us: I was asking her to walk away from a home that she and my late dad bought together and raised me in. It was the home where I learned to walk and talk. The home they'd finally paid off together by working hard all their lives, a year before my dad died. It was filled with Christmas and birthday memories, and the only home they'd ever owned. I felt terrible that I hadn't realized what I was asking of my mom, and sighed at the disappointment in myself. "Mom, I completely understand. Take all the time you need and enjoy your lunch. I'm going to the store to buy food for this weekend's dinner at Claire's."

After ending the call, a wave of guilt rushed through me, and I immediately called Slater.

"Hey babe. Everything okay?"

I flopped on the couch after putting Joy in the playpen with her sister. "Yes, I just needed to hear your voice. I just got off the phone with my Mom, and I feel awful."

Slater's concern could be heard in his voice when he spoke. "Is she okay? Do I need to come home?"

"She's fine, it's me that isn't doing so well. I've been so stupid and selfish; I could just kick myself."

"Honey, what are you talking about? Did you get into a fight with your mom?"

"No, I'm sorry. I mentioned the idea again of her and Lorenzo moving in with us because she hasn't said anything since she left, and she made me realize that it's more than that. I'm asking her to walk away from a house full of memories, one that she shared with my Dad, and I feel like shit for not realizing that."

"Oh baby, you only have your mom's best interest at heart. Don't beat yourself up over this. I'm sure your mom knows that. Don't try and rush her. I know you want to take care of her, but sweetheart, this needs to be your mom's decision, and she'll make the right one when she's ready, okay?"

"See, this is why I called you. You always know what to say and how to make me feel better. I love you. I'm going to pack up the girls and go shopping for Saturday."

"I love you too. Call me when you get back home."

"I will. Say hi to Ricky."

After ending the call I felt much better. I then proceeded to get the twins ready for shopping, and planned on picking up Scottie from school on the way home.

Shopping as usual was a challenge with just me and the girls and no Slater. The girls decided to be fussy at the checkout, and I was thankful that I remembered to bring two bottles of formula into the store with me and was able to calm them down when they began to fuss, sitting in their car seats in the double long cart. I was thankful Scottie was still in school and not with me. I was still haunted by the time he disappeared in the store before we left for our trip. The terrifying thoughts I had still clouded my mind, and today, being by myself with two fussy girls would have been a challenge to keep tabs on him too.

After arriving home with all three kids, Scottie pulled out his box of Legos and poured out the contents of the entire box into the middle of the room. I shook my head and rolled my eyes. "You make sure you pick up every single piece when you're done, Scottie," I said in a sharp tone from the kitchen as I put the groceries away, with Joy and Hope looking on from their playpen.

When I finally settled on the couch with a cup of tea surrounded by the kids and a Disney movie on TV, my phone rang. I saw it was Claire and immediately answered the call, and, as always, I was concerned about her pregnancy every time she called.

"Hey Claire, everything okay?"

She sounded happy on the phone. "Yes. We just got back from my weekly visit with the doctor. She said everything looks great. The baby seems to be doing fine, and I should breeze through the rest of the first trimester with no worries."

"Oh, that's fantastic news. Keep doing what you're doing. You looked great when I saw you. Pregnancy certainly agrees with you."

"I still can't believe it some days that I'm pregnant. I was told my entire life that the chances of me having a baby were pretty slim. Well, I proved them wrong," she laughed.

"You sure did."

"Oh, by the way, Sadie called me this morning to see how I was doing, and I told her about the dinner party; she and Logan will be there," Claire said.

"Oh great, thanks! I've not had a chance to call them. I've got everything we need for dinner, and we'll come over Saturday morning to start prepping if that's okay?"

"That's fine. It's been awhile since we've had a big dinner together. I'm looking forward to seeing everyone and meeting Dwayne and Tammy."

"Me too. I love our get-togethers. And our family just keeps growing."

"It sure does. Love you, girl. See you Saturday."

# CHAPTER 31

## SLATER

By the end of the week I'd had two more conference calls with Joseph. One was non-business related and had me somewhat excited when we ended the video chat. He'd called me to tell me that he knew of a house coming up for sale in the next week about twenty miles from where we were currently living. It was a five bedroom, three bath home with a fenced yard on a cul-de-sac. It sounded perfect, and big enough if Charlotte and Lorenzo decided to come live with us. It was also affordable, but as I listened to Joseph describe the house and location, I was excited on one hand, but still clung onto visions of Catalina Island and how perfect it would be to raise my family there, and that nothing I found here on the mainland would ever compare to it. I knew I had to let the crazy dream go, but I was having a tough time. Sabela, on the other hand, I knew would be excited, especially because it's big enough for our family, her mom and Lorenzo.

After ending the Zoom call, I locked up the trailer in the yard I rented where I kept all the tools and extra trucks, then locked the gates before heading home.

I found Sabela on the phone holding Hope when I walked in

the door. Scottie was in the middle of the room making funny faces at Joy, who was lying on her back giggling and squeezing Scottie's cheek. I smiled at the family atmosphere I'd just walked into and was reminded that it just doesn't get any better than this.

Scottie left Joy's side and raced into my arms as I put my ice chest on the kitchen table. Sabela spent a few more minutes on the phone and smiled at me from across the room, rocking Hope.

"Hey babe. Who was that on the phone?" I asked, picking up Joy who was starting to fuss since being abandoned by Scottie.

"My mom. I was checking in on her. How was your day?"

"It was good. Speaking of your mom, I spoke with Joseph via Zoom just before I left the yard, and he said he knows of a house that's going on the market next week."

Sabela's eyes lit up. "Really!"

I continued to tell her the size and price and that it was something we could afford. "I think we should take a look at it?"

"I sure wish my mom would make up her mind on whether she'd like to live with us. Five bedrooms is a big house if they don't."

After putting the girls in the playpen, I took Sabela in my arms and kissed her lightly on the lips. "What did I tell you about not pushing them? It doesn't do any harm to just check out the place."

Sabela wrapped her arms around my waist. "I know, I just wish I knew where we stood. It would be nice to know what size house we would need."

"Well, buying a house that's big enough will give your mom the option if and when she decides to live with us. In the meantime, it could be a playroom, an office. I don't know. It's only one room," I said with a slight edge to my voice.

As much as I knew that Sabela wanted nothing more than for her mom and us to be under one roof, Sabela's persistence was beginning to get under my skin, so I bit my tongue and let it slide before quickly changing the subject. "Come on, let's feed these kids, bathe them, and have a family movie night. Tomorrow morning I'll call Dwayne and Tammy and find out what time they'll be arriving, then we can head over to Claire and Travis' for the day. I'll wait until Monday to call Joseph about the house. I don't want to bother him over the weekend. It will be great to hang out with everyone. We've not done that in a long time," I told Sabela, kissing her on the lips.

Sabela smiled, which lifted my heart. "Sounds good. I'll let you and Scottie start the burgers while I take care of the girls."

***

I managed to get in touch with Dwayne early in the morning after having breakfast with the family. He and Tammy were also having breakfast at the Pancake Cottage on the island. I knew it well. Sabela and I ate there once, and they had the best pancakes. I envied them and let it be known.

"I'm sure the weather is perfect too," I chuckled. "I'm so jealous of you guys. I wish we were eating on that island with you."

"You're welcome anytime Slater," Dwayne told me. "We miss your company and look forward to meeting you and your friends tonight."

"That's why I'm calling. What time can we expect you? We're heading over to Claire and Travis' place in a little bit, we'll be there all day."

"We hope to be docked on the mainland by three this afternoon, and from there we'll take an Uber. We plan on spending the night on the boat after dinner, then driving it to our dock in Marina del Rey before we head out to our house in the mountains for a few days."

"You are certainly living the life, Dwayne."

"Oh, we've both worked hard all of our lives, now it's time for us to spend quality time with each other."

His words made me smile. "I love that. I gotta run, Sabela's calling me. See you tonight."

After ending the call, I heard Sabela call me again from upstairs. I raced up the stairs where I found her wrestling with Joy on the bed, trying to get her dressed, as Hope lay in the crib crying.

"Can you take care of Hope? I'm trying to get this one dressed, and Hope has no patience this morning. She probably needs her diaper changed."

I picked up Hope and immediately smelt the stench from her diaper. "Oh yeah, she's a stinky girl alright." I scanned the room. "Where's Scottie?"

"He's out in the backyard playing soccer." She picked up Joy and held her in the air. "Now aren't you the pretty girl, all dressed in yellow," she said, pulling her in and kissing her cheek. Joy smiled and let out a cute laugh.

An hour later at 10:00 am, with all of the kids strapped into their places in the back seat and the groceries for dinner in the cargo area, we were finally on the road to Claire's. I drove and Sabela texted Claire to let her know we were on our way. Then she made her usual morning phone call to her mom to check in.

"How's your mom doing?" I asked, after she'd ended the call.

"She said she feels great and will be at Claire's this afternoon around 2:00 pm."

When we arrived at Claire's, the house was already busy with the older foster kids, Jasmine, Nicole and Janet, who were helping Caroline and Abigail in the kitchen. Jasmine was helping Abigail cut fruit, and the two other girls were loading the dishwasher with Caroline.

Claire took Hope from my arms as she patted the top of Scottie's head. Then she called Travis who came in through the adjoining garage door.

He smiled and gave Slater a friendly hug. "Hey man, good to see you. Do you need help getting more stuff from your car?"

I nodded. "Sure, that'd be great. I'm not sure what Sabela packed, but there's a ton of stuff in the back of the car," I laughed, and then turned and looked at Scottie. "Come on buddy, you can help too."

When I came back into the house, I overheard Sabela talking to Claire about the house for sale.

Claire looked my way and smiled. "Slater, I hear you may have found a house? How exciting."

I forced a smile, unsure how I truly felt about the house. Every time it was mentioned, my Catalina dreams were being pushed farther away. I hated to admit it to myself, but a small part of me regretted telling Sabela about it. Maybe I should have waited a few days? I wasn't ready to let go of my dreams so quickly or discuss with my friends about moving into the suburbs.

"Well, we haven't seen it yet. It won't be on the market until next week," I replied, trying to act casual about the whole thing.

"You better jump on it fast when it is. The market's hot right now." Claire smiled, excitement reflecting in her eyes. "When are you going to go look at it?" she asked eagerly as Sabela looked at me with bright eyes.

"That's up to my new boss, Joseph. I'll give him a call on Monday. I don't want to disturb him over the weekend."

By 2:00 pm the house was bustling with all of our good friends. Ricky and Jill were outside entertaining the kids. Sadie was busy in the kitchen with Caroline and Abigail, while Sabela and Claire sat in the front room entertaining Joy and Hope, along with her mom and Lorenzo, while Travis, Logan and I sat at the kitchen bar having a beer.

"So, Claire told me you might have found a house," Travis said before taking a sip of his beer.

I released a heavy sigh. "We haven't seen it yet. It's not even on the market."

"Gotta be pretty exciting though, man. Your condo is getting pretty small now that you have the twins." Travis said, nudging my arm.

"Yeah, I guess."

Travis nudged my arm again. "Hey man, what's going on? You don't seem too excited. I've heard you two complain about the size of the condo before and that you couldn't wait to start house hunting."

"You'll have a much bigger backyard, too," Logan added.

Yeah, I know, and Sabela is super excited to go look at it. It's me that's holding back."

Travis creased his brow. "What do you mean?"

"I've got the Catalina bug," I laughed.

"The what?" Logan and Travis said at the same time.

"I can't stop thinking about that place, and nothing on the mainland does it for me. I can't shake it. I want to raise my family there, but the houses there are so damn expensive. I keep dreaming about it all the time. Day in and day out, it's all I think about."

"Damn, that's a pretty big dream. I hear those houses can cost a few mill," Travis said.

"You're right about that, but you know me - I always dream big. If I didn't, we wouldn't have this children's home, and I wouldn't be starting the biggest job of my career in a few months. To think, just a few years ago I traveled all over this state doing side jobs."

"Does Sabela know how you feel?" Logan asked, taking another sip of his beer.

"Yeah, I told her when we were on the island; she thinks I'm crazy and that I should just let it go."

"I hate to say it man, but maybe she's right?" Travis replied.

"Oh, I know she's right, but letting go isn't as easy as it sounds. I'm really trying man," I chuckled, finishing my beer. I was interrupted by a ding on my phone. I picked it up and saw that Dwayne had texted me and quickly opened the message. "Dwayne and Tammy are in the Uber and will be here within the hour, depending on traffic," I said, smiling.

"Great!" Travis said. "I can't wait to meet them."

"You're gonna love them. I'm going to tell the others and see if they need any help."

Dwayne and Tammy arrived forty-five minutes later, both dressed casually in denim jeans and white dress shirts. Tammy held a bouquet of mixed flowers which she gave to Claire, and Dwayne placed a delicious looking strawberry cheesecake on the kitchen counter.

"That's my favorite dessert! How did you know?" Claire laughed, peeking into the box.

"I think it's everyone's favorite," Tammy laughed. "One can never go wrong with cheesecake."

After shaking Dwayne's hand and giving Tammy a hug, I led them into the front room where everyone greeted them with friendly smiles and the chatter was plentiful. I knew from hanging out with them on the island that Dwayne and Tammy didn't drink alcohol, so I grabbed two O'Doul's from the fridge that I'd asked Sabela to pick up on her shopping trip.

"You remembered," Dwayne said with a look of surprise. "Thanks man, and cheers," he said, raising his bottle.

I raised my beer. "Cheers and welcome to the family. Everyone here is like family to us, and that now includes you and Tammy."

Tammy smiled and raised her O'Doul's. "Thanks. You guys are awesome."

After twenty minutes of standing in the middle of the room getting to know everyone, I took them outside to meet Jill and Ricky, who were still playing with the kids. Jasmine sat at the table next to Jill, where they were putting a scrapbook together of pictures of Jasmine's favorite animals that they'd cut out of magazines. I looked out on the grass and saw that Ricky was watching over the other kids playing on the swings and slides.

Jill looked up and smiled. "Hey, let me guess, you must be Dwayne and Tammy."

Dwayne chuckled. "We sure are, and you must be Jill."

"I sure am. We've heard so much about you two. It's great to finally meet you."

"And we've heard so much about all of you. Slater and Sabela raved about his family back home, and now I see why," Tammy said, taking a seat next to Jasmine. "What a pretty scrapbook. I love all the decorations on the pages," Tammy said, giving Jasmine a friendly smile.

"Thanks," Jasmine said in a shy voice, moving her body slightly closer to Jill.

Jill wrapped her arms around her shoulders. "It's okay, Jasmine. Tammy and Dwayne are our friends. They're going to have dinner with us."

"Cool," Jasmine said, gluing a picture of a bear cub onto a page.

While Jill and Tammy got to know each other, I walked Dwayne out onto the grass to meet Ricky, who was being chased by the younger kids led by Scottie. The laughter of happy kids filled the air, and Ricky raised his hands to end the game so he could talk to us.

"Ricky, I'd like you to meet Dwayne. His wife Tammy is talking to Jill at the table," I told him, laughing at the kids still trying to wrestle with him.

Ricky, out of breath, held out his hand and shook Dwayne's. "Nice to meet you. As you can see, I'm being attacked," he laughed.

Dwayne joined in on the laughter. "I can see that. What a wonderful place this is. I've heard so much about Open Arms. This is amazing, and such an incredible thing you're doing for these kids."

Ricky picked up Matthew, one of the youngest, who continued to tug at his jeans. "Thanks. We love them all. They brighten our day every single day. Why don't we head inside and see if we can help with dinner," Ricky said, rounding up the kids.

Dinner was served in the formal dining room where a massive mahogany table was the focal point of the room and seated every-one, including the children. Thankfully the twins were fed just before dinner was served and immediately fell asleep in the playpen.

Everyone helped with the setting of the table, bringing out the silverware and plates, and carrying all of the delicious food to the center of the table. Jill and Caroline sat at the end of the table where the children sat so they could help, if needed.

Once everyone was gathered around the table with their drinks of choice, I made a toast.

"Thank you everyone for joining us tonight. It's been awhile since we've all been under the same roof, and I really enjoy these times. I want to welcome Dwayne and Tammy to our family, and I hope they'll join us in many more future get-togethers. Sabela and I are so happy to have met you."

Dwayne smiled at the group as we all raised our glasses to welcome them. "Thank you, everyone. We've heard so much about all of you, and it's wonderful to finally meet you in person."

Tammy spoke next, smiling. "I can't tell you what a joy this is. The stories Sabela and Slater have told us have been wonderful to hear, and now I can put faces to all those stories." She laughed and looked at Jill. "I love that you and Travis used to date and have remained friends."

Jill looked over at Travis. "I care more about him now than I ever did when we dated," she laughed.

The entire table broke out into a roar of laughter. "And I love that you all came together and had a triple wedding," Tammy added.

"Well, Jill was a pain with her obsession with pink," Claire laughed. "But it was also a special day when Travis got to meet his mother Caroline for the first time," Claire said, smiling at Travis and then his mom Caroline.

Caroline smiled at her son and Claire. "Thank you Claire, for making it happen."

Jill commented next. "And if it wasn't for Travis' car accident, I probably would never have met Ricky." She leaned in and kissed

Ricky on the lips and then looked at Travis. "Sorry you had to go through that for me, Travis," she smirked.

The table erupted in laughter again as Travis raised his glass. "You're welcome, Jill," he said, with a smirk.

Tammy looked over at Sadie. "And you lived with Jill for a while before you met Logan."

Sadie nodded and smiled. "I sure did. She was the best roommate, and we had great times together, still do. She was with me the night I met Logan."

"You guys are awesome together, "Jill said. "I still can't believe you eloped." She giggled, her eyes bright.

We continued to share memories and laughter around the table, including Claire and Travis' miracle baby. The reunion of Claire and her mom Abigail. Davin the stalker, and Jill and Ricky's crazy honeymoon to Vegas, where he discovered his sister Anne was working for an escort agency. But because of Ricky's persistence and love for his sister, he managed to bring her back to San Diego, but not after she'd stolen $5,000 from them and almost burnt down their home. After that incident, Jill had had enough and insisted she should leave; a day later she was put on a plane to stay with her and Ricky's mother in Florida.

"How's she doing by the way?" Claire asked. "Have you heard from her?

"Funny you should ask, "Jill said. "I received a long apology letter from her just a few days ago. It was actually a nice letter, but not only that, she sent me a check for $1,000. She's working as a journalist for a newspaper and is keeping to her word and has started making payments for the money she took from us, as well as the money we loaned her."

"That's fantastic," Sabela added. "I'm glad to hear she's been able to turn her life around." She looked across the table at Ricky. "You saved her. You do know that, right?"

"I did what any big brother would do."

Over the delicious cheesecake dessert, the conversation shifted to Dwayne and Tammy, and how much they love Catalina Island, and how their big dreams finally came true.

"I know I've said this many times since meeting you, but I so envy you both. Raising my family on Catalina Island would be a dream come true," I said, my arm draped over Sabela's shoulder.

Sabela took my hand and rolled her eyes. "Oh, not that again. I thought we agreed that we could never afford to live there. I can't believe you're still thinking about it. A nice dream Slater, but totally out of our reach."

Dwayne intervened. "Not so fast Sabela, it never hurts to dream big. We always have and we followed those dreams, and to our surprise many have come true."

Sabela chuckled. "Dwayne, you're not helping. Whose side are you on?' she joked.

Dwayne hesitated before continuing. "Well, I'm not sure if this is the right time to mention this, but seeing how the subject has come up, I'm going to tell you anyway. I have a friend on the island that is looking to sell his family home, and I've told him about you and your family, and he's interested in meeting you."

My jaw dropped and the table fell silent.

Tammy took Dwayne's hand and smiled at us. "What do you say, guys?"

I was stunned about what I heard, and my voice shook when I finally replied. "I don't know what to say. This is unbelievable." I turned and looked at Sabela. "What do you think? You said you loved the island, and if we could afford it you'd love to live there."

The others at the table remained silent as everyone processed what Dwayne had said.

"Oh, I don't know Slater. This is crazy. What about your job, the construction business and then there's my mom? I'm not going to abandon her. You know how much I want to take care of her, more than anything." She looked over at Charlotte. "If she'll let me."

I wasn't ready to make such a huge decision in a matter of

minutes, but I did have some answers to Sabela's concerns, and in an effort to convince her that I could make this work, I began reeling off ideas, speaking excitedly and fast. "I could still keep the yard in town where our equipment and trailer are, and I could take the ferry to and from the island. It only takes an hour," I laughed. "Shit! I drive more than that in traffic to lots of jobs here in the city, and I can take an Uber to the yard where the trucks are stored, and, if necessary, I can spend some nights in the city." I paused to catch my breath and patted Sabela's knee. "We can still run S & S Construction, and I can still oversee my new job. As for your mom," I looked over at Charlotte. "She and Lorenzo can come live with us on the island, assuming the house is big enough. It would be a perfect place for all of us, but that would be up to your mom."

Suddenly my mom yelled out loud, startling all of us. "Do it, Sabela!"

Everyone at the table gasped.

"What Mom?" Sabela said, giving her mom a hard stare. "I'm not leaving you, Mom," she insisted.

"Listen to Dwayne. He's right. You must dream big. I can sell my house and you can use that money. It's paid for and it's worth to close to a million. That's a huge downpayment," Charlotte told her daughter.

Sabela's eyes grew wide, shocked by her mom's suggestion. "Mom, you are not going to sell your house, what are you saying. Stop it!"

Charlotte folded her arms across her chest and gave her daughter a hard stare. "I will not. It's my house and I'll do whatever I please with it. You're going to get it anyway Sabela, when I'm no longer here. Why wait until then? Enjoy the money now, I say. We can both enjoy it, Sabela."

Sabela looked at her, her brow furrowed. "What are you saying, Mom?"

Charlotte took a deep breath. "What I'm saying is, I want to sell my house and live out my remaining days with my family; you, Slater, Lorenzo and my grandbabies on Catalina Island. What you have told me about it sounds amazing, and I can't think of a better place to be and live out my life."

"But Mom, none of us have even seen the house."

Charlotte smiled. "Sabela, I don't need to see it, I'm quite sure it's magnificent. This is a big dream to fulfill; I want to be a part of it and help you achieve it. That's what moms do, Sabela," she chuckled. "Let me help you, and in return you'll be helping Lorenzo and I as we deal with this illness of mine one day at a time."

"Do it, guys!" Jill shouted from the other end of the table.

Sabela narrowed her eyes at Jill. "Hush Jill, I need to think." She looked at her mom with misty eyes. "But Mom, just the other day you told me your house holds so many memories of you and dad and that you weren't ready to sell. Why the sudden change of heart?"

"Because Sabela, this is a chance in a lifetime, an opportunity like this may never happen again, and yes, my house does hold many fond memories, but they're also in my heart, and they're not going anywhere. Wherever I go Sabela, I will carry these memories with me. I want to do this."

# CHAPTER 32

## SLATER

I grabbed Sabela's hand and squeezed it hard, my heart pounding in my chest. "Sabela, your mom's right. An opportunity like this may never happen again."

Sabela released a heavy sigh and looked at Dwayne. "Even with my mom's help there's no way we can afford a house on that island; please don't get Slater's hopes up, we've already been through this," she said rubbing her brow.

Dwayne raised his hand. "Hear me out, okay. Geroge is a dear friend of ours that we met many years ago. He's lived on Catalina Island for over forty years, raised his two girls there while he ran a well-established restaurant on the island. After he retired and sold the restaurant, he and his wife continued to live in their five-bedroom home after his two daughters moved out and began their careers in New York. One is an attorney and the other is in fashion design. Sadly, his wife passed away three years ago, and now his sister, who lives in Brentwood, is terminally ill. George also has some health issues and is finding it harder to live by himself in the big house, so six months ago he left and moved in with his sister so he can take care of her. He made the decision to sell the house, but only to the right people. He wants to sell it to a family that'll raise their children like he did his. He doesn't want to sell it to a developer who might tear down the house and build condos on the property; that happened to a few houses on the island. He refuses to go through a real estate agent and wants to sell it independently. He is not advertising that it's for sale. His exact words were, I will find the perfect family to buy my home. In the meantime, Tammy and I have been watching his property and maintaining it for him, and after meeting you and Sabela, I told him about you, your beautiful girls and Scottie, and what a wonderful family you are." Dwayne sported a large grin. "He wants to meet you. He's interested in selling."

I was stunned by what I'd heard.

"But what about his daughters? Why wouldn't he want to leave it to them? It is where they grew up," I asked.

"His daughters have no interest in the house, or even coming to California. They've made their lives in New York. George believes if he left the house to them, it would definitely be sold to a developer and be torn down. He refuses to let that happen. His daughters would be much happier with a check rather than the house," Dwayne laughed.

Jill spoke out again. "I think you guys should do it, and besides, I want to come stay at your house on Catalina Island."

Everyone at the table laughed. "Oh Jill, you always have a reason for anything that benefits you," Claire joked. "But all jokes aside," she turned and looked at Sabela and I holding hands, still in shock at the possibilities that'd just unfolded. "I think you guys should seriously think about it, and like Charlotte said, this is a chance in a lifetime, and if the island is as perfect as you've been telling us, then why wouldn't you?"

Sabela let go of my hand and rubbed her brow again. "Oh god, I wasn't expecting this at all. Yes, it's a beautiful place and perfect for our family. It would be like we're on vacation every day. It's safe for the kids, the school is small and there's very little crime, but we'd be away from all of you. We share our lives together and we are family, guys."

Travis spoke up. "And that will never change. You would be an hour away by boat Sabela, not halfway across the world, and I'm with Jill. I want to come hang out with you on the island, too. It would be a wonderful place to bring the children once Claire has the baby."

I sensed Sabela was feeling pressured, and she'd every right to be; this was my dream ever since we stepped foot on the island, and I wanted to make sure it was something she genuinely wanted too, not just fulfilling my dream. I turned and looked at Dwayne. "Would you mind if Sabela and I discussed this tonight when we get home and tell you tomorrow? This is a huge decision to make, and something we both must be on board with. I don't want Sabela to feel rushed."

"Of course. Take as long as you need, the house isn't going anywhere. I wouldn't expect you to decide tonight, but I did want to tell you about it."

Sabela released a sigh of relief and took my hand. "Thank you. This is a lot to take in, and we do need to talk about it and not rush into anything."

I gave her a caring smile and squeezed her hand. "I agree."

Jill spoke up. I assumed she'd persist with the idea that we should move to the island, but I was wrong.

"Well, if we're talking about life-long decisions," she took Ricky's hand and he smiled. "Ricky and I have an announcement."

Suddenly the room fell silent and then Claire squealed. "Oh my god, you're pregnant!"

Jill laughed, shaking her head. "No, I'm not pregnant."

Claire creased her brow. "Then what is it?"

Jill shifted in her seat and gave Ricky a loving smile when he gave her an approving nod. "Ricky and I have been talking about this for a few weeks, and the more we do, the more we're sure this was meant to be."

Claire leaned back in her chair, gripping the wooden handle. "Jill, you're killing me. What was meant to be?"

"Ricky and I would like to adopt Jasmine. We love her so much, and the thought or possibility that another family or couple could adopt her any day terrifies us. I can't imagine never seeing her again, and it scares the crap out of me that it could happen; I would be devastated."

Jaws dropped around the table and Jasmine looked up when Jill said her name.

Claire's eyes widened as she spoke. "Wow Jill, this is amazing! I know how close you and Jasmine have become. Her eyes light up every time you walk through that door." Claire shook her head and wiped a tear from her eye. "See, now you're making me cry. This pregnancy makes me so damn emotional."

Travis leaned in and hugged her. "I'm shedding a tear or two myself."

Jill stood and slowly walked around the table to where Jasmine sat, kneeling beside her and taking her hand. "Jasmine, do you understand what I just said?"

Jasmine looked at Jill with her innocent dark brown eyes and Jill ran her hand through her dark curly hair as she spoke. "You want to adopt me?"

"We do. Ricky and I love you very much, and we'd like to be your mommy and daddy. We want you to come live with us at our house."

"Everyday? I'd live with you every day?" Jasmine said in a soft voice.

Jill laughed. "Yes. We'd be a family. You would be our daughter." Jill smiled with tears trickling down her cheek, stroking Jasmine's cheek as she spoke. "Would you like that?"

Jasmine nodded, leaned in and hugged Jill as Ricky walked around the table to join them and hugged them both. "We love you so much Jasmine, and we never want to lose you," Ricky told her as he picked her up in his arms and spun her around.

"This is unbelievable," Sabela said. "I couldn't think of better parents for Jasmine. I've watched you three together and you already seem like a family. I see the love and trust between you, and in your eyes."

"I'll start the paperwork this week," Claire said, tears rolling down her cheeks.

I looked across the table at Dwayne and Tammy who'd been silent during Jill and Ricky's announcement as they witnessed a beautiful moment of friends coming together, like we always do.

"It's such an honor to be here this evening. This has turned out to be such a special night," Tammy said, raising her hand to her heart. "You are truly family. This is going to stay with me for the rest of my life."

Travis took Claire into his arms and kissed her gently on the lips. "We both dreamt big when we started this home with Sabela and Slater, wanting to save foster children from the system and give them a second chance in life. It was something I'd never experienced; I was in and out of foster homes my entire childhood until I ran away." He smiled at Claire. "Open Arms is doing what it was meant to do, and tonight Jasmine has found her forever family with Ricky and Jill. It doesn't get any better than this."

# CHAPTER 33

## SABELA

For the rest of the evening I was grateful the conversation shifted away from Catalina Island and instead focused on the group getting to know Tammy and Dwayne, as well as the big announcement about Jill and Ricky adopting Jasmine. I no longer felt pressured to make such a huge decision in a matter of minutes, and Slater was right; we needed to talk about it alone.

Jasmine was beaming when Ricky and Jill explained a bit more to her about how she would be living with them permanently and they'd be her new mom and dad forever, even when she was all grown up. Jasmine wouldn't leave their side for the rest of the night. It turned out to be a beautiful, memorable evening.

Before leaving and heading home, Slater promised Dwayne he'd call in the next day or so, after we'd had a chance to talk about the life changing choices we were now facing.

***

After thirty minutes spent tucking the kids into bed and

emptying out the car, exhausted from today's activities, we were finally alone, cuddling on the couch, relieved the house was quiet.

"That was quite the evening," Slater said, my head resting on his chest with his arm draped over my shoulder.

I looked up, stared into his eyes, and smiled. "It sure was. I knew everyone was going to hit it off with Dwayne and Tammy. How could they not? And Jill got super excited when Dwayne invited everyone for a fishing trip on their boat."

"Yeah," I laughed, tossing back my head. "And she'll probably show up with a pink fishing pole."

Slater let out a loud laugh. "You're probably right about that!" He paused; I knew what was coming next. "Have you thought any more about the house on Catalina?"

The moment had come. It was time to have a serious conversation about our future. I lifted my head from his chest and turned my body to face him, pulling my legs up and crossing them at the knees onto the couch. "I haven't stopped thinking about it since Dwayne mentioned it. Even with everything else going on around the table, it was constantly at the back of my mind. This is a huge deal, Slater."

"Yes it is, and like Claire and your mom said, a chance of a lifetime. We may never have an opportunity like this again. You know how I feel. I've not hidden how much I've fallen in love with the place. I've made that very clear, but after we saw that one house was selling for a few million, you convinced me that we could never afford anything there that could accommodate our family, plus your mom and Lorenzo. But things have changed, my big dream could actually become a reality."

I leaned back against the cushions of the couch and released a big sigh. "That's one of the things I love about you, you always dream big, and I feel a bit guilty that I tried to shut down your dream. I don't know what to do, I can't believe my mom is willing to sell her house and give us the money."

Slater rubbed my thigh. "I'm not surprised at all. You've been bugging her to move in with us, and, like she said, the house is yours after she passes, so it makes a lot of sense that she wants to do this for you." He squeezed my thigh again and looked me in the eyes. "Think about it, Sabela. Put yourself in her shoes. She doesn't know how much longer she has on this earth, and I think she looks at this as one final thing she wants to do for you and her grand-kids, and it will also allow her to be with you and the kids on a beautiful island 24/7."

Slater made a lot of sense, and I couldn't find any reason to disagree with him. It was my own fear of making such a huge move that held me back. I gave my forehead a vigorous rub with my two hands. "God, I don't know what to do, Slater. There is so much to think about."

"Like what?" he asked.

"Well, your new job, leaving our friends, and Scottie's school for starters."

"I already told you; I'd keep the yard and trailer and I could take an Uber to the trucks in the yard from the ferry. And as far as my new job, that doesn't start until March, so that will give us enough time to sell your mom's house and get settled on the island. As far as Scottie's school, I can guarantee that the one on Catalina Island is much better - smaller classes and a great envi-ronment." He squeezed my hand. "Can I remind you of the time we lost Scottie in the store and how scared we were? What was the first thing that ran through your mind when we couldn't find him?"

"That he was taken by a crazy person that may harm, or god forbid, kill him."

"Me too. That would never happen on Catalina Island. We wouldn't have to worry about our kids like we did that day. Crime is on the increase everywhere around here, in the cities and the suburbs. The schools have way too many kids in each class, and I'm constantly worrying about Scottie's safety. He doesn't have the freedom to ride bikes in the streets with other boys like we did growing up, or even play sports in the local park unless we're with him watching his every move. When I was his age, I'd walk to the park and meet my friends there, and on the way home, we'd stop and buy an ice cream. Catalina is so much safer for our children; the people are friendly, our kids would become well known, and I can guarantee you, other residents on the island would come to love them as their own and watch out for them, like all good neighbors do."

"But what about our friends?" I asked.

"What about them? You heard Jill, and I'm sure the rest feel the same way. Right now, we live thirty minutes away from most of them and rarely see them. If we're lucky, maybe once a week. I bet you we'd see them every weekend if we moved to Catalina. There's no better place to spend the weekend. I can just see Claire and Travis packing up all the kids, Jill and Ricky with Jasmine, and I know Sadie and Logan will visit often, because we both know how much Logan loves the water."

Slater nudged my shoulder. "Come on babe, what do you say? We've always dreamed big, now we have a chance of making one of our dreams come true. With your mom's help and a little bit of Eve's money, I bet we'll be able to afford to mortgage the rest. And don't forget, I'll be making good money with my new job."

My heart began to race with excitement. He was right about everything. I had no arguments. I would be a fool to turn this down. My heart continued to race as I gave him a big smile and took his hand. "Okay, let's do it, let's move to Catalina Island!" I squealed.

Slater eyes grew wide and his jaw dropped. "Seriously? Oh my god!" he yelled, taking me into his arms and kissing me hard on the lips. "You won't regret this. It'll be fantastic!"

I kissed Slater back before standing up and pacing the room. "I know. I've listened to everything you've said and you're right;

there's no better place for our family, and I'll be able to take care of my mom. I'm calling her first thing in the morning."

Slater left the couch and took me in his arms, then picked me up and swung me around, causing me to laugh out loud. "I can't believe it, we're moving to Catalina Island! I love you babe, with all my heart."

# CHAPTER 34

## SABELA

Seven Months Later

"Come on Scottie, grab your binoculars; Dwayne and Tammy just called from their boat and they're right outside the harbor," I said, as he struggled to put on his flip-flops.

"Yay! Are all my friends on the boat too?" he asked, picking up his binoculars from the coffee table. They'd become his latest obsession since we moved onto the island four months ago, before Slater started his new job, and it's been amazing. Scottie loves to sit on the beach with his binoculars and watch the boats come in.

"Yes buddy, Dwayne and Tammy have brought everyone to stay with us for a whole week. All the kids from the home: Colin, Matthew, Katie, Nicole and Janet. Daddy will have to go back to work on Tuesday, but he'll be home every night to spend time with all of us."

"Are Ricky and Jill coming with Jasmine?" Scottie asked.

I smiled. Jasmine had been living with them for almost three months, and I've never seen such a happy family. "They sure are, buddy. Sadie and Logan will be here too, and we're going to get to meet Travis and Claire's new baby boy for the first time. His name is Travis, too. They call him Travis Jr., isn't that cool?"

"That is cool!" Scottie squealed, his eyes bright.

I was ecstatic when I got the call from Travis two months ago that their son had been born by Caesarian section due to his whopping size which is quite common with a mother that had PCOS. My jaw dropped when he told me that he weighed a whopping ten pounds nine ounces. "Damn, he's a giant compared to my little girls when they were born two months prematurely and only weighed four pounds. Travis Jr. is like a three-month-old baby," I laughed. Up until the day he was born, I had called Claire every week to see how she was doing, and amazingly, she'd done great, with no complications.

A few months after we'd settled on the island, we packed the kids up, met with Dwayne and Tammy in the harbor, and headed over to the mainland on their boat to spend the day at Claire and Travis' home; Slater was right, it really wasn't that far, and it beat sitting in traffic whenever we had to commute to the mainland.

This will be the first time Claire and Travis will see our beautiful five bedroom home located up in the hills away from the busy part of the island where all the tourists congregate. Claire didn't want to travel while she was pregnant, and wanted to wait until Travis Jr. was at least a couple of months old before taking him on a boat. Jill and Ricky, along with Jasmine, Sadie, and Logan, have been here a few times on weekends, but it's been at least a month since they were here last. I swear I've seen more of them since we moved here than when we lived in the city. I chuckled at the thought because, yet again, Slater was right. He had predicted that before we'd moved here.

The house was perfect. I think we fell in love with it before we even saw it because it was on the island and affordable. George, the previous owner, came and met our family and made the decision that day that he wanted only us to buy his home and raise our family in it like he did. The transition was smooth, and we told George he was always welcome.

Having five bedrooms, Scottie has his own room, my mom and Lorenzo have theirs, and right now the girls are sharing a room until they get a bit older. We have the master bedroom, and the fifth bedroom is a guest room. The main floor is spacious with an open floor plan, with many French doors and large windows that bring in natural light and a gentle breeze when open.

A bonus we didn't expect was a finished basement, which we turned into a large office for our business.

It was decided that Claire, Travis and their son would stay in the guest room, and Abigail, her mom, would sleep on the foldout couch in our office.

Caroline and the rest of the kids from the home would be camping in the living room. Slater even mentioned setting up a few tents in the garden and having a campout with the kids for a few nights.

Jill and Ricky were excited to be spending the week on Dwayne and Tammy's boat, along with Jasmine. Sadie and Logan would just be here for the weekend and opted to stay in the hotel.

"Slater! Scottie is waiting," I called outside the French doors that looked out onto our spacious yard, enclosed by an attractive high rock wall that gave us plenty of privacy. "Dwayne and Tammy are right outside the harbor," I laughed, as the girls had recently turned one and were now walking. They were growing so fast, and I smiled as they sat on the grass with my mom and Lorenzo close by, rolling a ball around.

I smiled and waved at my mom drinking her morning orange juice. She loved the backyard, its shaded trees and comfortable lounge chairs on the patio area. It's where she spends most of her time reading, playing with the children, and most importantly, being with her family and allowing them to take care of her. She's doing okay. She has her bad days, but we're all here for her and cherish every day we have with her. The twins now call her nana and looked forward to her reading them a bedtime story every night.

Scottie tugged at my shirt as I stood in the doorway of the French doors. "Sabbie, is Daddy coming? I'm all ready."

I looked down and smiled at him, then looked over at Slater who was just ending a call. "Sweetie, your son's ready to go," I said with a grin.

"I'm coming," Slater laughed as he stood and headed towards Scottie. "Okay buddy, let's go meet the boat." He turned to me and kissed me softly on the lips. "We'll be back in about an hour."

"Sounds good. I can't wait to see everyone under the same roof again. It's been too long," I said, grinning.

After Slater and Scottie left in one of the three golf carts that we owned, I went and joined my mom on the grass with the girls.

"How are you doing today, Mom?"

She looked up and smiled as I took a seat next to her. "I'm feeling great. I think it's because I'm excited about seeing everyone again. This is going to be such a wonderful week with everyone here." She patted my knee. "See, I told you that you'd still see your friends. This is just the beginning, Sabela. You're going to make many fond memories here, and I'm so happy to be here enjoying it with you."

I squeezed her hand. "Me too, Mom. We couldn't have bought this place without you."

***

An hour later while feeding Joy and Hope bananas and apples in their highchairs in the kitchen, Scottie came racing through the doors, followed by Travis and Claire holding their new baby boy. I gasped and walked over to greet them, pulling back the light blue blanket from the baby's face.

"Oh my goodness, he's perfect, guys." I looked up at Travis. "He is the spitting image of you. He has your chin and cheekbones, and look at all that hair," I laughed.

Claire matched my laugh. "Right. Just like his dad, an abundance of thick hair."

"Slater's put one of the girl's old cribs together in your room, do you want to go lay him down in there? It's the first door on the right, upstairs."

Claire nodded. "That would be great. He just went to sleep." She kissed her son gently on the forehead and smiled. "I couldn't believe he was awake for the entire boat ride. He's probably worn out with so much to see. He was fascinated by the ocean. Travis held him up to the window and he was mesmerized for the entire ride."

As Claire ascended the stairs, I gave Travis a hug. "Congratulations, Travis. I know how much you and Claire have wanted this. He's definitely a miracle baby. I'm so happy for the two of you."

"Thanks. I still feel like I'm dreaming. Every time I look at my son, I have to pinch myself. It's an incredible feeling." Travis scanned the large open space where we stood and waved at Hope and Joy, who were pointing at him and smiling. "This place is amazing, Sabela. I can see why you moved here."

"Well, Slater was the one that dreamt big. I was a little reluctant at first, but not anymore. Anything is possible if we put our minds to it and never give up. Look at you and Claire. One by one your dreams are coming true. The children's home, you have a child of your own. What's next?"

Travis laughed. "You're right."

Slater joined us and looked over at Scottie, laughing with Joy and Hope as he handed one of them a slice of apple. "Hey Travis, do you want to follow me in one of the other golf carts down to the beach area where we're picking everyone up? It may take a few rides," Slater laughed. "My golf cart will seat six, but the other one only seats four."

"Sure, let me go tell Claire really quick and I'll be right out."

***

By lunchtime our yard was busy with all the familiar faces that I have gotten to call my family, including Jill and Ricky's dog Maggie and Claire's dog Tilly, who both did exceptionally well on their first boat ride. Slater, Travis, Logan and Ricky tended the barbecue, while Jill, Claire, Sadie and I and our moms entertained all the kids. We were enjoying watching Scottie being reunited with all of his buddies again, and playing ball with the dogs, along with Dwayne and Tammy's dogs, Tess and Miss Ellie. It was no surprise that Travis Jr. was the star that day, and everyone waited their turn to hold and cuddle him.

Dwayne and Tammy were now a part of our family and welcomed by everyone. We have shared so much in the short time that we've known them, and it's all because of them that our dreams have come true.

Laughter caught my attention, and I looked over at the grass where all the kids were playing tag with Dwayne, Ricky and Travis, as Logan served up the food from the barbecue onto platters with the help of Caroline and Abigail. It was a beautiful sight just to see everyone together again.

When we were all seated outside at the large table that Slater and the guys had put together, I pointed with my finger and counted everyone. We were a family of fourteen adults and nine kids. I was amazed at how far we'd all come and stuck by each other through thick and thin. Slater and I sat at the head of the table, with Joy and Hope on either side of us in their highchairs. Travis and Claire were on our right, and Travis Jr. slept soundly in his stroller. Next to us on our left was Dwayne and Tammy. Tammy soon got the table's attention when she tapped her spoon on her glass.

"Can I have everyone's attention?" she yelled, wearing a large grin.

I had no idea what she was about to say and raised my hands to quiet everyone. "Hush everyone. Tammy would like to say something," I hollered across the table.

The cheerful chatter around the table began to soften until there was complete silence. Tammy stood up.

"Thank you, everyone. I cannot tell you how honored Dwayne and I are to be here today and witness the reunion of all of you. You are all truly amazing. We have loved getting to know you and enjoy listening to all of your wonderful stories. In fact, if it's okay with all of you," she paused and smiled at everyone around the table then looked over at me, "I'd like to write your stories. I want to write about how you and Slater met."

She looked over at Claire and Travis. "I want to tell your story and the beginnings of the children's home, Open Arms." She then looked over at Jill and Ricky. "As well as your adventures in Las Vegas and little Jasmine." She then looked at Caroline. "I want to write about you and your son Travis finding each other. Then, looking at Sadie and Logan, "I can't forget about you two eloping." The table broke out in laughter. Tammy spoke up. "I love how you all have each other's backs, no matter what. Readers will grow to love you as I have. I would make it a series and call it the Sabela Series."

I gasped when she said my name. "You really want to tell our stories and name it after me?"

Tammy sat down and took Dwayne's hand. "I do. What do you think?"

Jill stood and raised her glass. "I love the idea!" She turned and looked at her husband. "Ricky, we're going to be famous!"

Again, the table roared with laughter and I smiled at Tammy. "I absolutely love it." I raised my glass to my wonderful friends and family. "Here's to the Sabela Series!"

"To the Sabela Series!" everyone yelled.

To say this is the last book in the Sabela Series is a bittersweet moment.

Slater book 1 was published in September 2019, almost four years ago. My intentions were to write a single romance novel while waiting for another book I had written to go through edits. Little did I know that the characters would completely take over, and that the Sabela Series would turn into an eight-book series with wonderful characters that I have loved getting to know and who have become a big part of my life over the past few years.

This series was such a joy to write. I'm going to miss it and the lengthy daily conversations I had with Slater, Sabela, Travis, Claire, Ricky, Jill, Logan and Sadie. I hope you have enjoyed reading it as much as I have enjoyed writing it.

This final book, Dream Big, was a crossover, with Tammy Mellows from my trilogy, The Tammy Mellows Trilogy and her husband Dwayne meeting the characters in the Sabela Series.

If you've read the Tammy Mellows Trilogy, then you know Tammy and Dwayne are based on my husband Gordon and I. Let me tell you, I had so much fun putting ourselves into a fictitious world that I had created with characters that over the years have become real to me, and in the book, we are living the big dream that we share in real life if we ever strike it rich, while encouraging Slater and Sabela to follow theirs. It was truly a wonderful experience to write this book.

Thank you for reading my books, and I can't wait to tell you what's coming next.

Until then,

Happy Reading!

Love,

Tina xoxo

# ALSO BY TINA HOGAN GRANT

**THE TAMMY MELLOWS SERIES**
**<u>First Fall - The Prequel</u>**
**<u>Reckless Beginnings - Book 1</u>**
**Better Endings - Book 2**
**The Reunions Books 3**
**Waves And Memories - A Short Story Collection**

**THE SABELA SERIES**
**Davin - Prequel**
**<u>Slater - Book 1</u>**
**<u>Eve - Book 2</u>**
**Claire - Book 3**
**Jill - Book 4**
**All Of Us - Book 5**
**Vegas Bound - Book 6**
**Open Arms - Book 7**

# ABOUT THE AUTHOR

Award-winning author Tina Hogan Grant was born in England and moved to the States in 1979. After moving to California, she became a commercial fisherwoman and spent ten years fishing off the southern coast of California with her husband Gordon. After retiring from fishing, they moved to a small mountain community in CA and spent the next ten years building their dream home, doing most of the work themselves.

Grant enjoys writing suspense romances, stories with strong female characters who know what they want and aren't afraid to chase their dreams.

Favorite quote: "There's no such word as can't "

When Grant is not lost in her world of writing she enjoys riding ATVs, hiking and discovering new trails, and going on long road trips.

Grant's book Better Endings won a gold medal award for Best Fiction Adventure 2020

And The Reunions won a Gold medal award for Best Fiction Adventure 2021

Grant has had appearances on FOX NEWS Bakersfield, Bakersfield NOW NEWS, HOMETOWN -KVPA Radio Santa Clarita, Voyage LA Magazine, and The Mountain Enterprise Newspaper.

Keep in the loop with Tina and receive Davin The Sabela Series Prequel for FREE by signing up for her newsletter https://www.subscribepage.com/tinahogangrant